Take a chance on love....

"See? Chivalry isn't dead after all," Professor Louis Miles said.

Jessica's heart began to pound. Why did he have to be so gorgeous? "Chivalry may not be dead, but it's definitely on sick leave," she said harshly, surprised by the sound of her own voice.

Louis's forehead wrinkled. "Oh, c'mon. you seem too young to be so bitter."

Jessica felt herself opening up, ready to tell him anything he wanted to know about her life. "I've been hurt too many times. Whenever I thought I'd found true love, it turned out there was nothing real about it. I've given up on love altogether."

"Don't do that—" he said with an urgency that caught her off guard. "The worst thing you can do is lose hope."

Their eyes locked. His green eyes stared at her with such an intensity, Jessica couldn't seem to break away. She felt as if they were drawing her down further into their swirling depths.

Does he feel it too? she wondered. Jessica's head was spinning. She wanted to believe that Professor Miles was attracted to her, but what if she was wrong? She had to find out. Her heart wouldn't survive another break.

SWEET VALLEY UNIVERSITY®

Behind Closed Doors

Written by
Laurie John

Created by
FRANCINE PASCAL

BANTAM BOOKS
NEW YORK · TORONTO · LONDON · SYDNEY · AUCKLAND

RL 6, age 12 and up

BEHIND CLOSED DOORS
A Bantam Book / October 1995

Sweet Valley High® and Sweet Valley University®
are registered trademarks of Francine Pascal
Conceived by Francine Pascal
Produced by Daniel Weiss Associates, Inc.
33 West 17th Street
New York, NY 10011

ISBN: 0-553-56695-4

Published simultaneously in the United States and Canada

Bantam Books are published by Bantam Books, a division of Bantam
Doubleday Dell Publishing Group, Inc. Its trademark, consisting of the
words "Bantam Books" and the portrayal of a rooster, is Registered in
U.S. Patent and Trademark Office and in other countries. Marca
Registrada. Bantam Books, 1540 Broadway, New York, New York 10036.

PRINTED IN THE UNITED STATES OF AMERICA

OPM   0 9 8 7 6 5 4 3 2 1

To Daniel Pepple

Chapter One

There must be some mistake. Jessica slammed the door of her mailbox and read the letter again. She wanted to believe it had been slipped into her box by accident—that it belonged to someone else. But the cold black type at the top of the page proved her wrong. The letter was addressed to *Ms. Jessica Wakefield.*

It was Friday morning, and the Sweet Valley University Student Union was jammed with students. Many of them stopped by to check their mail or to go to the campus bookstore. Others hung out in the lounge to talk about what was going on for the weekend.

Jessica stuffed the letter back into its envelope. "I can't believe this is happening," she said, groaning as she made her way across the crowded mail room over to where her twin sister stood. Jessica cringed when she spotted Elizabeth's outfit of baggy denim overalls and a floral-print T-shirt.

"Milking the cows early this morning?" Jessica said dully as she brushed the lint off her black slip dress.

"I'm going to ignore that," Elizabeth answered calmly. She was busy sorting through an enormous stack of letters that filled her mailbox. "Get anything good?" she asked as she tore into an envelope.

Jessica leaned heavily against the wall of mailboxes and let out a loud sigh. "Actually, Liz, something terrible's happened," she said, fanning herself with the envelope.

Elizabeth looked up from the letter she was reading, her blue-green eyes darkening. "What's wrong, Jess? Did something happen to Mom and Dad?"

Jessica rolled her eyes. "No, no—nothing like that." *Liz can be so dramatic sometimes,* she thought. Jessica unfolded the letter and waved it in front of Elizabeth's face. "Take a look at this."

Elizabeth quickly glanced at the paper. "It's a registration slip for a seminar—what's the big deal?" she scoffed, shrugging.

Jessica tossed a lock of golden blond hair impatiently over her shoulder. "The big deal is that Isabella and I signed up for the History of Film seminar so we could be in a class together. All you have to do is show up for class, watch a movie, then leave. It's the perfect seminar." The corners of Jessica's mouth turned down as she pointed to the print at the bottom of the letter. "But look what they gave me instead."

Elizabeth's eyes narrowed as she read it. Suddenly a bright smile broke over her face and she started to laugh. "*Now* I know why you're so upset."

"It's not funny, Liz." Jessica pouted. "I don't know a thing about medieval history."

"Well, Jess, it looks like you're about to learn." Elizabeth patted her sister on the shoulder sympathetically. "Who knows? Maybe you'll actually like it."

Jessica crossed her arms in front of her and scowled. "Not a chance. There's no way I'm sitting through some boring class, listening to a dorky professor lecture about stuff that happened hundreds of years ago. *You* might go for that kind of thing, but *I* have better things to do."

"Like watching old movies?" Elizabeth teased. She eyed the clock above the main entrance. It was almost nine thirty. "Speaking of boring lectures, I'd better get going or I'm going to be late for mine." Elizabeth piled the stack of letters into her leather backpack and swung the bag over her shoulder. "Cheer up, Jess. It's not the end of the world."

Yeah, right, Jessica thought gloomily. She forced a smile and waved good-bye to her sister. Elizabeth headed toward the glass doors, books in hand, blond ponytail bouncing as she walked. *She may be the optimistic one, but at least I have all the fashion sense.* Jessica crumpled the registration slip into a ball and tossed it into her shoulder bag.

A steady stream of students were coming into the building, flooding the already crowded foyer of the union. Jessica decided to leave before she was

3

trapped in the mail room. She headed toward the front doors, weaving through the oncoming crowd. Just as she was about to step out into the bright sunlight, she spotted Randy Mason coming up the path.

This day is getting worse by the minute. Jessica jumped back and pulled the door closed. *I hope he didn't see me,* she thought as she spun around on her heels. She turned to face a wall of people blocking her in every direction. She was trapped.

"Excuse me!" she said, trying to shove her way through, but no one moved. Randy had reached the entrance and was walking through the door. Jessica quickly reached into her shoulder bag and pulled out a black straw hat and a pair of sunglasses. She tucked her long blond hair up into the hat, pulling the brim down low. Then she slid on the shades, which turned everything in the room pitch-black.

Jessica's pulse raced. People moved in behind her, pushing her along as the crowd moved forward. She felt like a tightly coiled spring that was about to be released. When the mob gave way, Jessica blindly plowed forward, heading in the direction of the back door.

"Jessica?" a voice called directly in front of her.

Jessica's heart leapt to her throat. She lifted her head slightly and slid the shades down to the tip of her nose. "Isabella!" she whispered with relief. "I'm *so* glad to see you!"

"Let me guess." Isabella Ricci's gray eyes surveyed Jessica's outfit. "You're rushing off to a fashion show in Paris, and you want me to go with you."

"I wish," Jessica scoffed. She slowly turned and looked over her shoulder. "Actually, I'm hiding from Randy."

Isabella scanned the crowd. "Why are you hiding from your boyfriend?" she asked, puckering her glossy red lips.

Jessica pulled the hat down around her ears. "We can't talk here; it's too dangerous." Reaching for Isabella's wrist, she led her out the back door. Once they were safely on the outside steps, Jessica took off her hat and threw it into the bag. "He's not my boyfriend anymore."

Isabella's gold bangles tinkled as she threw her hands up in the air. "What happened? I thought you were thrilled to be reunited with your long-lost love from middle school."

Jessica shrugged. "I was at first. But it just wasn't working out," she said simply. She untangled her hair with her fingers. "I kept seeing him as the same nerdy little kid I knew in sixth grade. So I broke up with him last night."

Isabella arched one perfect eyebrow. "That must've been a shock. How did he take it?"

"I think he'll be okay." Jessica looked across the campus to the clock tower at the end of the quad. "I'm trying to avoid him for a few days. You know, lay low until things smooth over."

Isabella's red mouth twisted into a wry smile. "So who is it now?"

"What do you mean?" Jessica answered defensively.

"You know exactly what I'm talking about." Isabella playfully tugged at a hoop earring. "Who's the new man in your life? I've never seen Jessica Wakefield close one door unless another one was about to open."

Jessica pursed her lips thoughtfully. "There isn't a new man in my life," she said in a firm voice. "And there isn't going to be one, either."

"Stop joking. I know you better than that."

"I mean it. I'm through with love—it never works out," Jessica said honestly.

"Don't say that," Isabella cooed. She put a consoling arm around Jessica's shoulders. "I know things have been tough for you lately, but you just haven't found the right guy. Someday, when you least expect it, you'll bump right into him and that will be it—you'll live happily ever after."

Jessica shook her head doubtfully. "Only in fairy tales, my dear," she answered. "My life is a total mess."

They started walking toward the quad. "You sound like you need some cheering up," Isabella said sweetly. "Are you going to Theta house right now? Maybe I could do your nails—I just got this great kit for French manicures."

"Maybe some other time," Jessica said grimly. "Right now I have to head over to the registrar's office to straighten out another mess in my life. Remember that seminar we signed up for? I didn't get it."

Isabella frowned. "That's a real bummer, Jess. That class won't be half as much fun if you're not there. Is there any way you can change it?"

"I sure hope so. If not, I'm going to be stuck taking Medieval History for the rest of the semester."

Isabella laughed sympathetically. "That sounds terrible. Go over there right now and show them who's boss."

"Thanks for the pep talk." Jessica smiled tiredly. She turned and headed down the path leading to the administration building. "I'll catch up with you later."

"What about the Xavier Hall party tonight?" Isabella called. "Are you going?"

Jessica sighed. "Are any cute guys going to be there?"

Isabella laughed. "I'm sure there will be—it's in honor of Craig Maser. The entire wrestling team will probably be there."

Jessica threw her bag over her shoulder and walked faster toward the administration building. "Then I guess you'd better count me out."

Todd Wilkins yanked his Lakers poster off the wall of his dorm room and tore it in half.

"What are you doing?" Gin-Yung Suh got up from the couch and walked over to where Todd was standing.

Todd threw the pieces in the trash can. "I don't need any reminders. I don't want anything to do with basketball anymore."

He looked up at his trophy shelf. The gold, gleaming figures that lined the shelf stared back at him indifferently. At one time the little statues had meant so much. Now he saw them for what they really were—pieces of molded plastic and cheap metal. Todd put his hand at the end of the shelf and with one sweeping gesture pushed all the trophies off the shelf into the cardboard box waiting below.

"Don't do this to yourself, Todd," Gin-Yung said as she watched him seal up the box.

Todd's eyes were wild. "I'm not the one who's doing it. *They* did this to me." He reached into his closet and pulled out his prized possession. The orange, textured surface of the basketball felt strange to his touch. He knew every scratch and mark on that ball, the exact spot where it would balance perfectly on his fingertip. They had been through everything together. Yet now his prized basketball seemed foreign and distant to him. As though it belonged to someone else.

Todd gently squeezed the ball between the palms of his hands. A hard, bitter lump formed in his throat. "I want you to have this," he said hoarsely. He tossed the ball to Gin-Yung.

She looked at Todd with sad eyes, the corners of her mouth turned down. "You know I can't take it."

Todd looked away. "I don't care what you do with it. Just get it out of my sight."

"Don't let them do this to you, Todd. If you give up, you're just letting them win."

Todd angrily kicked the trophy box. The lump in his throat burned. "They've already won."

Gin-Yung patiently took the ball and tucked it away safely under Todd's bed. He didn't protest.

Todd gave the box another kick. He felt like a rubber band that had been stretched to its limit and at any moment would snap. "I guess Mark Gathers made the right decision after all," he said. "Maybe I should've left when he did."

Gin-Yung pulled Todd away from the box and sat him down on the couch next to her. "Don't give up, Todd. There has to be a way out of this. Think."

"There's nothing to think about." Todd hung his head. "I got a letter from Coach Crane—the head of the athletics department. He won't let me rejoin the basketball team. My career is over. End of story." The words echoed endlessly in his mind.

"I'm sorry. But there must be something we can do," Gin-Yung answered softly. She wrapped her arms gently around his neck. "Did he give you a reason?"

Todd shook his head. "Not really. The letter said 'it isn't possible at this time.' I don't get it. Coach Shultz, from Sweet Valley High, said that if I wrote a letter of apology to Coach Crane at the end of the season, asking to be reinstated, it wouldn't be a problem."

"That's really weird," Gin-Yung said. "Did you talk to Coach Crane himself?"

"Not yet." Todd touched his cheek against Gin-Yung's silky black hair. "I don't know if I even want to." He stood up and began to pace the

9

room. "I've always thought the punishment Mark and I got was too harsh anyway. All the blame was dumped on us. It was the department that gave the star players special treatment—we just accepted it."

He stared into Gin-Yung's dark eyes. In them he could see that she didn't need any persuading; she already believed him completely. Somehow he still needed to say the words aloud, as if to convince himself. "I know it wasn't fair to the other players, but I've already served my time. So why won't they let me come back?"

Gin-Yung sighed. "What are you going to do now?"

"I don't know."

She walked over to the window where Todd stood and rested her hands on his shoulders. Todd's muscles relaxed under her touch. "Why don't you come out with me tonight? There's a big party at Xavier Hall. It might take your mind off things."

Todd kissed her tenderly on the forehead. "You go ahead without me," he said, his voice cracking as he spoke. "I need to be alone."

Winston Egbert's ears rang as he listened to the booming voice on the other end of the telephone line. Occasionally he had the urge to remind his father that his hearing was perfectly fine, but Mr. Egbert rarely gave Winston the opportunity to speak. Instead Winston resorted to keeping the telephone receiver several inches away from his ear or swinging it in circles above his head. Still, he could hear every word his father said.

"Son, did you hear what I just said?" Mr. Egbert asked. He had a habit of asking Winston questions to make sure he was paying attention.

Winston stopped in mid-swing and brought the receiver to his mouth. "Yes, Dad," he answered mechanically.

"Your mother and I are very proud of you. Last semester's grades were terrific," Mr. Egbert repeated.

Winston flinched as the sound reverberated in his ear. "Thanks," he answered meekly. Suddenly a tightness seized his chest, as if his muscles were twisting themselves into hard, ropy knots. He couldn't catch his breath.

Winston dropped to the floor, his back flat against the blue-and-white throw rug. He was having a panic attack. It happened whenever he was stressed, and usually when he was talking with his father.

"It's no accident that you've been doing so well. I know you've been working hard for those grades."

Winston coughed loudly. He set down the phone receiver near his ear and stretched his arms high above his head. He inhaled slowly through his nose and exhaled slowly out his mouth. It was a breathing exercise Denise had taught him to use whenever an attack came on. Winston took another deep breath.

"Your mother thought that when you started dating Denise, your grades might suffer." Winston heard his father laugh. "I said to her, 'Don't worry, Winston's got a good head on his shoulders—he can handle it.'"

A guilty pain shot through Winston's rib cage. His dad had no way of knowing what was really going on in Winston's life, yet he always managed to hit a nerve. It was as if he knew Winston hadn't turned in his last three physics assignments because he'd spent every waking moment with Denise. It was the first time Winston had ever been in danger of failing a class. "Actually, Dad, my classes have been a lot tougher this semester," Winston breathed into the receiver. "My grades might not be so good this time around."

"Nonsense. I'm confident that you will do just fine," his father answered. "Your mother and I couldn't be happier."

The tightness in Winston's chest was beginning to spread throughout his whole body, gradually squeezing the air out of him. He took in several quick, deep breaths, cupping his hand over the end of the receiver so his father wouldn't hear. Winston decided that there was no point in trying to tell his dad the truth; he didn't want to hear it.

"Good luck on your physics exam, although I'm sure you won't need it."

"Thanks," Winston wheezed into the receiver. "I'll talk to you later." He hung up before he heard his father say good-bye. Winston lay on the floor for several minutes, staring up at the white ceiling. *What am I going to do?* he wondered. If he was forced to take the exam at this very moment, there was no doubt in Winston's mind that he would fail. But the test was two weeks away, and he knew that even if he crammed every night until then, the best he could hope for was a C. Winston could see an image of his parents as he continued to stare up at the ceiling, their eyes filled with disappointment when they discovered that their son had failed the physics exam. Winston felt faint.

Think positive, Winston told himself as he stretched his hands high above his head again. Denise told him once that whenever he wanted to reach a goal, all he had to do was imagine himself achieving it. "If you have a positive attitude, you're more than halfway there," she had said.

It sounded a bit simplistic, but it was worth a try.

Winston took a deep breath and imagined himself sitting in the auditorium of the science building with the test in front of him. He saw himself answering all the questions easily, one right after the other. He would be the first one in his class to finish the exam. And then he could see Professor Stark's stony face break into a smile as he shook Winston's hand. "Well done, Mr. Egbert," he'd say.

There was a knock at the door. Winston felt himself being reluctantly being dragged back to reality. "Winnie, are you in there?" a sweet voice called from the other side of the door.

"Come in!" Winston answered, the knots in his

muscles beginning to unravel. Denise strode into the room. Her hair was pulled back into a loose bun, and she wore a faded SAVE THE EARTH T-shirt with a pair of faded jeans and an old plaid shirt tied around her waist. She was beautiful in a completely unselfconscious way. The sight of her made Winston feel as though he could melt right into the rug.

"What are you doing on the floor?" Denise asked, staring down at him with amusement in her brilliant blue eyes.

"I thought I dropped something, but I guess not." Winston hopped clumsily to his feet, his cheeks turning an embarrassing pink. He was such a goofball that he often wondered what Denise could possibly see in him. He wasn't used to having beautiful women interested in him. Sometimes Winston felt as if Denise were somehow misled, that she honestly believed she was dating someone worthy of her. He knew it was only a matter of time before she found out the truth.

Denise looked at him strangely. "I just wanted to remind you that the party starts around nine tonight, so be ready to go at eight thirty."

Winston looked at her blankly.

Denise rested her hands on her hips. "Winnie! Don't tell me you forgot about the party!"

"Oh—I didn't forget," he lied. He'd been so preoccupied with worrying about the upcoming physics exam, the party had slipped his mind. "What is this party for again?"

"I can't believe you. This is the biggest party of the semester, and you're probably the only person on campus who doesn't know anything about it." Denise sighed. She moved a pile of dirty clothes and plopped down onto his striped futon. "Let's start from the beginning. Do you know who Craig Maser is?" she said with a deliberate tone.

Winston rolled his eyes. "Of course I do—he's the star of the baseball team."

"Wrestling."

"Huh?"

Denise crossed her legs impatiently. "He's the star of the *wrestling* team. I swear, Winnie, sometimes I think you live in a cave."

"May I remind you that it's the same cave you live in," Winston said with a smirk. Actually, Winston thought of Oakley Hall as being more like an exotic tropical island. It was an oasis where he was surrounded by beautiful women who were constantly fawning over him. Although there were many advantages to being the only man in an all-women's dorm, Winston sometimes felt isolated from the masculine elements on the campus. "So what does Craig Maser have to do with the party?"

Denise untied the plaid shirt that hung around her waist and put it on. "To make a long story short, Craig Maser was chosen to go to Las Vegas for this big wrestling match that's going to be televised on the new NCAA cable network. Tonight there's going to be a huge bon voyage party for Craig at Xavier Hall," she said matter-of-factly. "So when will you be ready?"

Winston stared at the unopened physics book sitting on his cluttered desk. His muscles tensed. With all the studying he had to do in the next few days, the last thing he should be doing was going to a party. "Denise, I'm so sorry, but—"

"But what?" she asked expectantly.

Winston looked deeply into her eyes and instantly knew how much she was looking forward to the party. His heart ached at the thought of disappointing her. "I don't know."

Frown lines appeared on Denise's forehead. "You don't know what?"

Lines appeared on Winston's own brow as he shoved his physics book into a desk drawer. "I don't know if I can be ready by eight thirty," he stammered. "How about nine?"

Denise's face brightened. "Well, that's no problem, Winnie. Whenever you're ready, just holler. You know where to find me." She stood up and gave Winston a quick kiss.

Winston watched her leave, her movements as fluid and graceful as a willow tree bending in a summer breeze. He sat at his desk, rested his head on his arms, and closed his eyes, the softness of her kiss lingering on his lips. He had a few hours before the party. There was still time to get a little studying done. Winston opened the desk drawer and looked at his physics book, dread bearing down on him like an iron weight.

*   *   *

Elizabeth spotted Tom near the front entrance of the ivy-covered English department building. He was facing the opposite direction, toward the library. She snuck up behind him and playfully covered his eyes. "Guess who?" she said, disguising her voice.

Tom reached up and touched her hands. "Could it be that gorgeous redhead I met in the coffeehouse this morning?" he answered.

Elizabeth dropped her arms, resting her hands on her hips. She eyed him suspiciously. "What *redhead*?"

Tom looked at her with mock surprise. "Oh, Elizabeth, it's you! I had no idea—" He laughed.

"I don't think it's a wise move, Mr. Watts, to make your girlfriend nervous. Especially when you're about to leave for Las Vegas for two weeks." Elizabeth laced her fingers with his.

Tom pulled her close to him and gave her a long, slow kiss. "You can tell my girlfriend that she has absolutely nothing to worry about. I'll be way too busy to get into any trouble."

Elizabeth's stomach did a somersault. Part of her was still reeling from his kiss, but a larger, deeper part of her was frightened at the thought of him leaving. They had never been apart for more than a few days since they first started going out. Up until now, everything had been perfect between them. She hoped nothing would change.

"I'm a little nervous, though," Tom said as he gave her shoulder a squeeze. "I'm not crazy about

17

leaving you here alone on a campus with tons of single guys."

Elizabeth smiled coyly. "Don't worry," she reassured him. "I'll be so busy thinking about you, I won't have time for anyone else."

Elizabeth hugged him, resting her cheek against his shoulder. She watched the last few students in her English Composition class enter the building. The green door closed, and the walkway that had been so full of activity a few minutes earlier was suddenly quiet. "I'd better go," Elizabeth said. She pulled away and gave him a soft kiss. "I'll see you at lunch."

Tom still held on to her arm as she started to walk away. "Wait—I can't meet you for lunch. I'm spending the whole day at WSVU. I have a ton of work to finish before I leave."

Disappointment flickered in her blue-green eyes. "What about tonight? You're going to the party, aren't you?" she asked hopefully. "After all, you're the person who's going to Las Vegas to broadcast the wrestling match. It wouldn't look too good if WSVU's senior correspondent didn't show up for Craig Maser's party."

"I'll go, but I might be a little late. I'll meet you there." Tom flashed her a sexy smile. "Save all the slow dances for me."

Chapter Two

"Hello? Is anyone here?" Jessica called from the front counter of the registrar's office. The place was a disaster. Cardboard boxes were stacked on desks, and files and computer equipment were scattered all over the floor. No one was around. The entire office looked as though an earthquake had just hit and everyone had run for cover.

"This has got to be *the* worst day of my life," Jessica said aloud as she squeezed the crumpled seminar slip in her fist. *They must've known I was coming,* she thought angrily. But they couldn't avoid her forever. Someone had to show up sooner or later, and she'd be right here waiting for them. She'd wait here until Monday morning if she had to. There was no way she was going to get stuck taking Medieval History.

Jessica propped her elbows on the counter and waited. A few minutes later a student worker appeared in the doorway, carrying a large file box. "Can I help you with something?" he asked her. He dropped the box on the floor and grinned at her. Jessica thought he had a very cute smile.

"Actually, you can," Jessica answered anxiously, sauntering over to the door. She gave her hair a casual flip. "This will only take a second." She uncrumpled the ball of paper and waved it in front of his face. "There's a mistake here. I signed up for History of Film and somehow I ended up with Medieval History. I guess you guys got your histories messed up." Her voice was as smooth as velvet.

He laughed a deep, genuine laugh. "The film seminar is a popular course—unfortunately there wasn't enough space for all the students who wanted to take it. So we had to place you wherever there was space available. . . ."

"And I'm sure there was plenty of space available in Medieval History." Jessica pouted. "Why don't you just sign me up for something else?"

His eyes took in every detail of her face. "Normally I would, but as you can see, we're in the middle of moving things around for the campus renovations. Right now our computer system is down, and it won't be up and running again for a few days."

"A few days? But this class starts tomorrow!" Jessica snapped. She noticed that one of his front teeth was chipped.

His smile faded. "Take this," he said flatly, handing her a form. "It's a drop form. Have your professor sign it, and when the computers are running, we'll put you on a waiting list for another seminar. In the meantime you'll have to go to the class you're signed up for."

Jessica's face flushed with embarrassment. She shoved the form into her bag and stomped out of the office. She was wrong to think that imbecile would be willing to do a simple favor for her. The more Jessica came in contact with men, the more convinced she was that she wanted nothing to do with them.

Lila Fowler held up her perfectly manicured right hand for her Theta sorority sisters to admire. "Isn't Isabella marvelous?" Lila said.

"Exquisite," Alison Quinn said as she inspected Lila's nails. "You should start your own business, Isabella."

"Thanks," Isabella said humbly as she added a clear coat of polish to the nails on Lila's left hand. "But I only do this for fun, not to make money."

Magda Helperin took a seat at the dining-room table near Isabella. "If you're not interested in making money, you could always donate it to charity. We could set up a booth for you outside the house just before the spring formal."

"You could become our official Theta fundraiser," Alison added, playing with the ends of her silk scarf.

Isabella giggled. "I think I'll pass."

"Leave the poor girl alone. She's not a workhorse,"

Lila interjected. She turned to Isabella, her voice softening. "Don't sell out, darling. If you want to give manicures for fun, I'll always be here to support you."

Kimberly Schyler dropped an armful of books on the table. "And whenever Lila is too busy with that boyfriend of hers, you can count on me to help out."

Isabella guided Lila's wet fingertips to the nail dryer. "Just how is Mr. Patman these days?" she asked with a sly grin.

Lila's face glowed. "Bruce is wonderful. I couldn't be happier," she said, holding back a laugh. The words sounded strange even to her ears. Lila had known Bruce for years, and he was the last person she had any intention of falling for. But life took people in unexpected directions, and here they were, totally in love. Lila was convinced that even if they hadn't been in a plane crash and lost in the wilderness, something else would have brought them together. They were simply meant to be.

"Is he coming to the party tonight?" Isabella asked.

Lila nodded, her eyes sparkling.

Kimberly twirled a curl around her finger and laughed. "Have you ever heard of the Sigma president missing a party? The whole fraternity is going to be there."

"I guess that means all the Thetas will be there too," Magda said.

Isabella closed her makeup case. "Everyone except Jessica, that is."

Lila lightly touched her nails to check if they were dry yet. "What do you mean?"

"Jess asked me if any cute guys were going to be there, and when I said yes, she said 'Count me out,'" Isabella answered.

"That doesn't sound like the Jessica we all know and love," Alison said sarcastically. Alison had never liked Jessica, and she made no attempt to hide her feelings. "You sure you weren't talking to Elizabeth by mistake?"

Isabella threw Alison an exasperated look. "I think I know when I'm talking to Jessica," she said harshly. "She just doesn't feel like going out, that's all."

"You have to admit it does sound a bit odd. Jessica never misses a party," Lila said, gesturing with her elegant hands. Her eyes narrowed suspiciously. "My guess is that she's got something better up her sleeve."

Winston stood on the side of the stage and straightened his tie, waiting to be introduced. The lights in the auditorium dimmed, and a hush fell over the crowd.

The president of the university spoke. "Tonight it is a great honor to present to you one of Sweet Valley University's most distinguished alumni. He has studied astrophysics and quantum mechanics at both Harvard and Oxford Universities, and has written more than forty books on his research. Currently he is using his expertise to redesign NASA's space program.

23

Tonight he will be giving a talk entitled 'Einstein's Theory of Relativity: What's Wrong with It.' It is a privilege and an honor for me to introduce this great man to you all. Ladies and gentlemen, please help me give a warm welcome to Dr. Winston Egbert."

Winston walked out into the spotlight and shook the president's hand. The crowd was instantly on its feet, cheering, applauding. He had the admiration of everyone in the room.

"Thank you. Please, please sit down," Winston said modestly.

When the room quieted, he began.

"First, I wanted to thank you all for coming here tonight."

The crowd was completely still, hanging on his every word. His parents were sitting in the first row, directly in front of the podium. His father beamed proudly and winked at Winston whenever he looked his way. His mother smiled broadly, dabbing an occasional tear that came to her eye. And, of course, there was Denise. She was still as beautiful as when they were in college. She looked up at him adoringly.

He finished his speech to a thunder of applause. Even the Sigmas, who had tortured him during the fraternity rush, were on their feet, clapping. The days of Winston Egbert the clown were over; now he was respected and admired.

The president motioned to a microphone at the front of the stage. "If any of you have questions, please come forward."

A young man walked to the front of the stage.

24

"Since you're talking about Einstein, Dr. Egbert, can you please tell me what the E stands for in $E=mc^2$?"

"Certainly," Winston answered confidently. "It stands for explosion."

A blond girl in the middle of the crowd stood up. "That's not right!" she shouted. "It stands for energy."

Winston nodded. "Yes—yes, of course it does. She's absolutely right."

The young man returned to his seat.

A man in the back row stood up and walked down the center aisle toward the front of the stage. He was Winston's college physics professor. His hair was completely white, but Winston recognized the stern expression and the polka-dot bow tie.

"Dr. Stark, it's a pleasure," Winston said, holding out his hand to shake.

The old professor ignored Winston's gesture and just nodded. "Dr. Egbert, I think the crowd has treated you a bit unfairly, asking you questions that seem to be out of your realm of knowledge. But I do have one question for you, concerning the study of black holes."

Winston relaxed. He was an expert on the subject. "Please, sir, go ahead."

"I'm sure you must have heard about the group of students at U of O who recently sighted a black hole through their telescope. What did you think of that?"

Winston scratched his chin in a scholarly manner. "Actually I did hear about it, and I think it was a wonderful discovery."

The crowd roared with laughter. A few people pelted him with paper airplanes.

"What's wrong? What did I say?" Streams of sweat poured down Winston's face.

The old professor was laughing so hard he was having trouble breathing. "It was a trick question. You can't see a black hole. Maybe if you had done your work when you were in my class instead of spending all your time with Denise, you'd know the basics."

The crowd ran for the door.

"Don't go!" Winston called after them.

His own father left with the mob, too ashamed to be seen with his son.

His mother came forward, tears streaming down her cheeks. "Even I know that you can't see a black hole," she said softly, unable to look him in the eye.

Denise stepped forward. She looked at Winston for a moment, then slapped him hard across the face. "I'm leaving you," she said as she stormed out, slamming the door behind her.

The room was empty. Winston felt totally alone. Suddenly there was a knock at the door.

"Winnie, are you in there?"

There was another knock.

Winston opened his eyes slowly. His vision was blurry, but as it cleared he suddenly became aware that it had all been a terrible dream. Sometime during the afternoon of studying he had dozed off with his head on the physics book.

"I'm coming . . ." he said groggily as he lifted

his head. He had fallen asleep with his mouth open, and a puddle of drool had accumulated on his open book. Winston wadded up a piece of notebook paper to clean up the mess.

"Winnie, are you ready yet?" Denise called from the hallway.

"No." He opened the door. Denise stood before him, looking totally gorgeous in a red knit minidress.

"You promised you'd be ready at nine," Denise said. She brushed back a piece of his hair that was sticking straight up. "What happened to you? You look like you fell asleep in a pile of newspapers. You have ink all over your cheek."

Winston groaned, wiping his cheek with the back of his hand. "I'm sorry. I was studying, and then I guess I dozed off. Give me ten minutes and I'll be ready."

Denise went off to wait in the lobby. Winston tore through his closet and ran to scrub the ink off his cheek. He was suddenly very glad to be going out with Denise, especially since she looked so beautiful in that dress. It didn't matter that he didn't get any physics problems done. At the moment, the thought of anything related to science made him completely sick to his stomach.

"Are you sure you don't want to go to the party, Jess?" Elizabeth asked as she laced up her black ankle boots.

"Positive," Jessica answered from behind a

fashion magazine. She glanced up at her twin and studied the outfit she had changed into. It was better than farmer clothes, but it was still a far cry from fashionable. "You're wearing *that*?" she said with disdain.

"What's wrong with what I'm wearing?" Elizabeth answered defensively. She inspected her black jeans and tapestry vest in the mirror.

Jessica tossed the magazine aside and strode over to her side of the closet. "This is a college party, Liz—not an ice-cream social. Live a little."

Elizabeth watched her sister rummage through the pile of clothes that were heaped at the bottom of the closet. "Keep that mess off my side, please," she said. She looked at herself again in the mirror. "I like what I'm wearing. I'm comfortable."

Jessica sighed. Sometimes she couldn't believe they'd both come from the same gene pool. "If comfort is what you're after, why don't you just go to the party in your pajamas?" She grabbed a burgundy silk blouse off a hanger and tossed it at Elizabeth. "Tom's leaving tomorrow for Vegas, right? Don't you want to knock his socks off so he won't forget you?"

"It's not like he's going away for six months. It's only a few weeks." Elizabeth held the blouse against her body.

"You know what they say—out of sight, out of mind." Jessica tossed a pair of black stiletto heels in her direction.

"Cut it out. It's hard enough that he's leaving;

I'm not going to spend my time worrying. I trust him completely," Elizabeth answered firmly. She pointed to a picnic basket on her desk. "It's not like I'm not doing anything romantic for him before he leaves. I went to the gourmet shop to pick up a few things for a moonlight picnic on the quad later on." She touched the soft, flowing sleeves of the blouse. "Maybe I *should* dress up a bit."

"That's my girl!" Jessica shouted. She helped Elizabeth slip the blouse over her head.

Elizabeth clutched the front of the blouse in alarm. "Isn't this thing cut a bit too *low*?"

Jessica looked at her strangely. "What do you mean? It's perfect." She returned to the pile at the bottom of the closet. "I have a sequined miniskirt that would look terrific with that. If only I could find it. I know it's somewhere in here. . . ."

"This is fine, Jess, really—" Elizabeth waved her hands in protest. "I'll just put on some mascara and then I'll be ready to go."

Jessica shrugged. "If that's how you want it." She abandoned the search and threw herself onto her bed. "But you've got to lose that ponytail."

Elizabeth yanked the elastic out of her hair and snapped it at her sister. "Are you satisfied now?"

Jessica nodded. "You look absolutely gorgeous—just like someone I know."

Elizabeth laughed as she ran a brush through her long golden hair. "So what's on your agenda tonight?"

"Since you're wearing *my* clothes out, I thought

29

I'd stay in and pretend to be *you*," Jessica said casually.

"You're not going out with Randy?"

Jessica shook her head. "Randy and I called it quits," she said, her voice even.

Elizabeth stopped brushing and looked at her sister. "Oh, Jess—I'm sorry to hear that. Are you all right?"

"Fine. It's no big deal," she said nonchalantly. She scanned the books on Elizabeth's shelves. She pulled down a copy of *Ulysses* and started to thumb through it. "Is this any good?"

Elizabeth looked at her with suspicion. "Okay, Jess—what are you up to?"

Jessica squinted as she tried to read the tiny print. "Nothing, I swear."

Elizabeth carefully applied mascara to her lashes, making sure it didn't go on too heavy. "I know something's up. For one, Jessica Wakefield has never missed the opportunity to go to a great party, and two, she has never expressed a curiosity in reading James Joyce."

"Stop badgering me." Jessica fluffed up her pillow and slid underneath her purple bedspread. "Maybe I'm tired of the social scene. Maybe for once I'd like a quiet evening alone with a good book."

"Right!" Elizabeth grabbed her keys off the rack she kept by the door. "Whatever it is you're planning to do tonight, just make sure it's legal."

"Whatever you say, Mom . . ." Jessica called as Elizabeth closed the door. She sighed contentedly. *Alone at last.*

Jessica pulled the covers up to her chin. No sound came from the hallway. Everyone was gone. She was glad that Elizabeth was going out to-night, but she didn't envy her one bit. Dating and relationships were definitely overrated. If she had decided to go out, Jessica would've spent hours putting together a devastating outfit and making sure her hair and makeup were just right. And for what? Just so her heart could be smashed to pieces a few weeks or months later? Falling in love was a dangerous proposition, and she had the scars to prove it.

Jessica picked up the magazine again. Of all the wounds she'd suffered from love, her failed marriage to Michael McAllery cut the deepest. At first she thought of it as just an error in judgment—an honest mistake. But then there was James Montgomery. When they'd started dating, Jessica had been certain he was the most perfect man she had ever met. A few weeks later he had almost raped her. Then he'd denied it.

Jessica decided that romance just wasn't in the cards for her. There was no way she was going to let herself be vulnerable ever again. Even if that meant going through the rest of her life totally alone.

31

Chapter Three

Music pounded from a row of giant speakers at the front of the room, rattling the walls and floor of Xavier Hall until it seemed ready to shake off its foundation. Blue, orange, red, and green lights swirled and pulsed in time to the music. Dozens of white balloons covered the ceiling, and a banner with the words CONGRATULATIONS, CRAIG MASER was suspended above the crowd. Even though the doors had been open for only a few minutes, the dance floor was already crammed with students, their arms lifted high in the air as they moved to the beat.

Occasionally an elbow or an arm would hit Lila in the back, but she hardly noticed. All she was aware of was the gorgeous guy who held her in his arms. Lila put her head on Bruce's muscular shoulder, and they swayed slowly to their own rhythm. It didn't matter to Lila that they were slow dancing in the middle of a very crowded and noisy Xavier Hall. They could have been in a grand European ballroom dancing a Viennese waltz and she wouldn't be any happier.

Bruce bent his head and whispered in her ear. The sensation sent shivers through her whole body.

"Are you having fun?" he asked softly.

Lila's lips twisted into a wry smile. She ran her glossy fingertips through his thick hair. "What do *you* think?"

Bruce's perfect white teeth glowed from the black light. "You look like you're having fun to me." He kissed her on the forehead. His brown eyes stared into hers for several long, romantic minutes. "Lila, there's something I've been wanting to tell you."

"And what's that?" Lila answered, completely mesmerized by his gaze.

Bruce gently toyed with a lock of her hair. "I've had this on my mind for a long time, and I've finally decided to do something about it. I'm going to move off campus."

Lila's body stiffened beneath his touch. "What do you mean?" she squeaked.

"I like living at Sigma house, but there just isn't enough space. I'm sure you know what that's like from being in your dorm. Besides, now that I have money from the trust fund, I can afford a place of my own." Bruce spoke as if he had weighed the matter seriously and his mind was already made up.

Lila pulled Bruce closer to her. Even though he would be only a few miles away, it felt as though he were planning to move across the ocean. Lila couldn't imagine what it would be like without having Bruce right there when she needed him. She wouldn't be able to stop by Sigma house and see him between classes or pick him up for an early morning cappuccino. Without Bruce around, she'd be lost.

"I'm tired of living on campus and eating in the dining halls. I want a place on the beach where I can get away from everything."

Including me, Lila thought gloomily. The more he talked about it, the more she realized he was right. Living off campus did sound wonderful. She couldn't really blame him for wanting to leave. "Sounds good," she said, looking away.

"You don't seem very enthusiastic." Bruce tilted Lila's head so she was once again staring right at him. "I was hoping you'd be excited."

"I am," Lila said, tears of disappointment stinging her eyes. "I'm just going to miss you, that's all."

Bruce smiled patiently. "Lila, you're missing the point." He brushed back the hair from her eyes. "I want you to come *with* me. I thought maybe we could get a place together."

Lila stared at him for a moment, the words slowly turning around in her mind. *He wants us to move in together.* Instead of sitting in her room feeling lonely, she would be with Bruce in a glorious house by the ocean. They would spend their

34

days at the beach and sip champagne by the fire every night. Lila couldn't imagine anything in the world that could be more romantic.

"Oh, Bruce! I'd love to!" Lila squealed, nearly jumping into his arms.

"But there is one thing I'm worried about." He looked at her intensely, lines creasing his brow. "I know that Tisiano made a very comfortable life for you. I want you to be happy—to have everything you want. I have quite a bit of money, but I can't compete with an Italian count."

Lila smiled. Her brief marriage to Tisiano had been nothing less than magical. They had lived in the most beautiful villa on the Mediterranean Sea, and she had been pampered by servants. After Tisiano was killed in a tragic boating accident, Lila returned to Sweet Valley and resumed her life as it was before. She held the memory of Tisiano close to her heart, but somehow it all faded into the distance, like a spectacular dream. Sometimes Lila felt it had all happened in another lifetime. She was no longer the Countess di Mondicci—she was Lila Fowler. And she was with Bruce now.

"I don't care if we have to live in a coal mine," Lila said as she held him tight. "I just want to be with you."

Elizabeth closed the door to the telephone booth to block out the noise that was coming from the party. "What did you say?" she shouted into the receiver.

35

"I said I'll try to be there, but—" Tom was saying something, but there was too much interference. Elizabeth couldn't hear a word. Just as she was about to ask him to repeat it, she heard the coins drop inside the pay phone and the line went dead.

"I hope he doesn't take too long," she said to herself. Since Tom was leaving tomorrow, she was hoping they could have a romantic evening together, but the night was almost half over. She crossed her arms in front of her, touching the silky sleeves of the blouse she had borrowed from Jessica.

Elizabeth watched the party through the glass door of the booth. Without Tom, she really didn't want to hang around. *Don't wimp out,* she scolded herself. *Just go and have a good time—he'll be here soon.* Besides, Nina and Bryan were supposed to be there. She could stick with them until Tom showed up. She opened the door to the telephone booth, the roar of the crowd hitting her like a tidal wave.

Elizabeth impatiently brushed back a strand of hair that kept falling in her face, wishing she'd kept her hair in a ponytail instead of listening to her sister. The temperature on the dance floor was unbearable from the hot lights and the crush of dancing bodies.

The room suddenly went dark, then someone turned on a strobe light, making the crowd scream. Everyone seemed to be moving in staggered slow motion, like extras in a modern Charlie Chaplin flick.

Elizabeth edged along the wall to avoid being jabbed by flying elbows and knees. She squinted into the flashing lights, but she couldn't really tell if Nina and Bryan were there. She looked around the room for a familiar face, someone she could talk to while she waited for Tom. There were a few people she recognized, many of them members of the Theta sorority. No one she really cared to start a conversation with.

The music stopped suddenly, drawing a chorus of boos from the dancers. Elizabeth took advantage of the motionless crowd to slip past them over to the punch table on the other side of the room. Her ears felt as if they'd been plugged with cotton balls.

"May I have your attention, please," a voice cut in over the loudspeaker. It was Jay Knox, president of the Zeta fraternity. Cheers came from a group of Zetas gathered in the corner, and Jay raised his hands to quiet everyone down. "Thanks for coming out tonight. As you all know, one of SVU's top athletes has been chosen to represent our region at a wrestling match in Las Vegas."

Elizabeth reached for a paper cup and filled it with punch. *Tom should be here,* she thought. He deserved the same amount of recognition that Craig was getting. Just as Craig was chosen among the best wrestlers in the country for this big match, Tom was among the top college journalists in the country chosen to cover the event. Elizabeth looked up at the huge banner hanging over her head and the cocky faces of the Zetas. Tom would never ever have let someone do all this in his honor. It just wasn't his style.

"This match is going to be televised all across the country on the new NCAA sports channel. Our campus station, WSVU, will be covering the event. I hope all of you will tune in and show your support for this great athlete—Craig Maser. We're proud of you, buddy."

Craig walked up to the stage, waving his thick, muscular arms at the crowd. Whistles and applause came up from the students. A cheerleader who was standing next to Elizabeth jumped and did a split in midair, knocking Elizabeth's punch all over the silk blouse she was wearing.

My sister's going to kill me! Elizabeth thought with dread, sopping up the liquid with a few napkins. She could feel the dampness against her skin, but the colored lights made it impossible to tell just how bad the stain was. Elizabeth pushed her way across the dance floor and headed to the bathroom.

She blinked a few times from the harsh fluorescent lights of the ladies' room. When her eyes adjusted, Elizabeth stared at her reflection in horror. There was a dark splotch on the burgundy silk, the liquid spreading through the fibers.

"This is a disaster," Elizabeth said aloud, grabbing a stack of paper towels and running them under the faucet. Just as she was about to rub the stain with wet towels, Elizabeth heard someone

38

gasp. It was Gin-Yung, Todd's new girlfriend.

"Don't do that," she said as she took the towels away from Elizabeth. Gin-Yung rolled up the sleeves of her white blouse. "Rubbing will only make it worse." She grabbed a few dry towels and carefully patted the blouse. "Just try to absorb as much of the liquid as you can."

"Thanks," Elizabeth said gratefully. She thought it was strange that Gin-Yung was being so kind to her. It was rare to find someone who was willing to talk to their boyfriend's ex, not to mention help her out. Obviously Todd had found someone very special. "This just might come out after all," Elizabeth said with relief as the patch got lighter. "Thanks so much for your help—I really appreciate it."

"Anytime," Gin-Yung said. The floor started to vibrate as the music kicked in. "Sounds like the party's rolling again."

"Yeah. What a great party," Elizabeth said with a sarcastic note in her voice. So far the evening was a complete success. Not only did none of her friends show up, but her chances of having a romantic evening with Tom were diminishing every second.

"Is Tom here?" Gin-Yung asked.

Elizabeth shook her head. "He's still at the station, finishing up some work before his flight tomorrow."

"I can't believe the cable network invited all those college journalists to cover the event," Gin-Yung said enthusiastically. "And Tom gets to do the live broadcast of Craig Maser's wrestling match. He's so lucky."

He is lucky, Elizabeth thought wistfully. But she knew that it was much more than luck that gave Tom this wonderful opportunity. He had drive and talent. She was tempted to tell Gin-Yung how proud she was of him, but she didn't want to be impolite. "And how's Todd?" she asked.

Gin-Yung frowned. "He could be a lot better. He didn't come tonight because he just found out that Coach Crane won't let him back on the team."

Elizabeth's jaw dropped. "That's crazy," she cried. "Todd's one of the best basketball players at SVU!"

"I know—he had the best shooting average of anyone on the team. It doesn't make any sense to me either. Todd's taking it so hard." Gin-Yung stared down at the floor. "I feel so helpless. I wish there was something I could do."

"I know what you mean," Elizabeth said thoughtfully. When she first broke the story of the athletics department granting special favors to its star athletes, Elizabeth had no way of knowing how much Todd was going to be affected by it. Even though Todd had accepted privileges, he didn't deserve to be punished so severely. It was almost as if the department was making Todd their scapegoat. "What's Todd going to do?"

Gin-Yung knelt down to tie the laces of her Converse high-tops. "Nothing, I'm afraid. I think he's disillusioned with the entire program."

Elizabeth bit her lip, frowning. It wasn't like Todd to give up without a fight. He couldn't throw everything he'd worked so hard for down the drain. She wouldn't let him do it.

A warm breeze danced across the dark quad, and Jessica took in a deep breath of the fresh air. It smelled slightly salty, like a gust of clean ocean air off the nearby Pacific. She glanced up at the bright full moon, its silvery beams casting a glow on the campus. It was the kind of night that was perfect for a romantic walk along the beach. Jessica closed her eyes, felt the warm wind blowing through her hair, and saw herself walking barefoot in the cool sand. She imagined the hush of the rolling surf at low tide. Beside her was the most incredible man she had ever seen. He gazed at her with longing, then took her in his arms and . . .

Just stop it right there, Jessica Wakefield, she said to herself, interrupting her own thoughts. She opened her eyes and hurried across the quad. She had done it again. *You are such a sap.* The whole reason she had taken a walk in the first place was to keep her mind off romance, and here she was, fantasizing again. *There's no point in wasting time thinking about something that only ends up bringing you pain,* her mind said. But even after all she had been through, Jessica's heart was still searching for the romantic ideal.

Staying alone in her room had been fun at first, but the novelty quickly wore off. Jessica threw on a pair of jeans and a pullover and decided to look for something to do. The problem was finding something to do that didn't involve romance. It was a lot more difficult than she'd imagined.

As she wandered down the shadowy paths of the campus, Jessica began to realize just how limited the possibilities were. Craig Maser's party was definitely out. She had thought about stopping by the coffeehouse, but she might see Randy there, and that was the last thing she wanted. Then of course there was the snack bar, but that was a favorite hangout of the football team, and she might run into James. It was better to stay away.

The lights of the Student Union glowed up ahead. "I suppose I could check my mail again," she said glumly. It was the only option left. She suddenly wished she had brought her straw hat and sunglasses along with her. She'd hate for anyone to see her checking her mail on a Friday night.

As Jessica approached the building, she noticed that the campus bookstore was still open. *Who would hang out at a bookstore on a Friday night?* she wondered. Jessica pictured dorky science students shopping for calculators and antisocial people glancing through books in the aisles. She stood outside, debating whether or not to go in. What if someone saw her?

Don't be silly, she told herself. *No one you know is anywhere near this place.* It was either kill some time in the bookstore or spend the rest of the evening alone in her room. Jessica went inside.

The thick, fragrant aroma of coffee hit her as soon as she walked through the door. "Would you like a cup?" a young woman asked from behind the counter. "It's free to our Friday night customers."

"No thanks," Jessica said. She was tempted to take some, but she was afraid of suddenly having a connection with *one of them*—those strange people who spent prime party nights in the campus bookstore. They were there because reading was their life. She was only there because she had nothing better to do.

Jessica looked around. A few people were milling about, leafing through textbooks or shopping for stationery. None of them looked out of the ordinary or sorry that they were missing some big social event. In fact, they all seemed content, absorbed in whatever it was they were doing.

No one noticed her. Jessica smiled. Maybe this wasn't so bad after all. She had found something to do without being bothered by anybody. And she certainly wasn't in any danger of finding romance in the bookstore.

Jessica wandered aimlessly through the aisles, trying to find something that sparked her interest. She walked over to the textbook section, finding the shelf where the History of Film seminar books were kept. She touched the glossy cover and flipped through the thick pages. The book was loaded with pictures of movie stars, and Jessica sighed as she looked at all the beautiful photographs. Her favorite chapter had pictures of all the glamorous actors and actresses from the forties. Jessica loved the elegant hairstyles and beautiful clothes. But most of all, she loved the handsome leading men.

Jessica wistfully put the book back on the shelf. Isabella was lucky. The film seminar was going to be an amazing class. Unfortunately Jessica's chances for getting into it were incredibly slim.

Directly above her was the Medieval History shelf. She reluctantly glanced at the seminar textbook. The cover had a photograph of an old tapestry showing two knights in armor fighting on horseback. The book was unbelievably thick, and Jessica had to use both hands to pick it up. She thumbed the pages and curled her upper lip in disgust as she scanned the tiny print.

"I take it you don't like medieval history," a deep voice said.

Jessica looked up. Standing beside her was a tall young man with wavy golden brown hair and green eyes. He was dressed conservatively, in a brown tweed blazer and loafers. She was taken aback. She had never seen someone so gorgeous dressed in such boring clothes. "How can you tell?" she asked.

"Oh, I don't know," he said. The corners of his perfectly shaped mouth turned up in a smile. "Maybe it was the look of horror on your face."

Jessica smiled politely. "I had no idea I was so obvious." She dropped the heavy book back onto the shelf. "Unfortunately it looks like I'm going to be stuck taking it anyway. The seminar I wanted is all filled up." She hadn't wanted to get entangled in a conversation with anyone. Suddenly Jessica realized she was telling this stranger more than she had intended, but she couldn't stop herself.

"What class did you want to take?"

She pointed to the book. "History of Film."

He picked up the film book and looked at it closely. Jessica couldn't tell if he was being serious or just joking as his eyes scanned the pages. "I can't believe students take courses for something they can rent at their nearest video store instead of learning about something new and different."

Jessica choked back a giggle. Judging from the intense expression on his face, this was no joke. He meant every word he was saying. "What's wrong with taking a class in something you're interested in?" she argued playfully. "There are enough boring classes out there—so you might as well take something fun."

"Fun is a state of mind," he said, his full lips curving into a smirk. "With the right approach, any subject can be interesting."

Jessica looked at him sheepishly. "Somehow I doubt that."

"It's true," he persisted. "Take medieval history, for example. It just so happens that it's one of my favorite subjects—"

"I feel sorry for you," Jessica teased. This guy was gorgeous *and* brainy. Not exactly Jessica's type, but certainly the kind of guy her sister would go for. Too bad Elizabeth was taken—Jessica had found the perfect man for her.

He laughed good-naturedly. "Don't be. It's a fascinating subject—and I'm certain that even you would find it interesting."

Jessica tossed back her hair. "I hate to break it to you," she answered resolutely. "But I will never be interested in that subject."

His smile disappeared, his green eyes widening. "Oh, no—you said that *word*."

"What word?" Jessica was absolutely confused.

"Never," he whispered, leaning toward her. "This is a very grave situation. Do you know what this means?" He shook his head as if he were trying to comprehend it. "Whenever you say the word *never,* it always comes back to haunt you. You've just sealed your fate. You're about to become a medieval history fanatic!"

Jessica clamped her hand over her mouth to keep from laughing aloud. He was probably the strangest person she had ever met, but also the most intriguing. "If you only knew me," she said, smiling brightly. "You would never think that I would be a fanatic about any academic subject."

"Why not? You seem to be a very clever, intelligent person. There's no reason why you couldn't be interested in studying history."

Color rose to Jessica's cheeks. *Clever? Intelligent?* Those were words people used to describe Elizabeth. No one had ever said that about Jessica. When he looked at her with his sparkling green eyes, did

46

he see something in her that no one else did?

"You don't look convinced. I guess I'll just have to prove it to you." His strong, well-shaped hands reached for a book. "If you give me one minute, I bet I can make you interested enough in medieval history to at least go to the first class."

Jessica arched one eyebrow skeptically. "This should be interesting, all right." She looked at the wall clock. "You have exactly one minute. Starting . . . now."

He started in immediately. His voice was calm and easy, as if he went door-to-door selling medieval history books for a living. "There are elements to medieval history that are just as interesting as any of the classic movies. Arthurian legends are loaded with heroes and heroines, passionate love stories, battles between good and evil." He flipped through a few pages. "Who is one of your favorite classic film actors?"

Jessica thought quickly. "Fred Astaire."

"Good choice," he said with a smile. "If you like Fred for the same reasons I do, you like him because he is graceful and elegant—a true gentleman. Am I right?"

Jessica nodded. That was exactly why she liked him.

"The same can be said of men in the Middle Ages. Believe it or not, the knights were very socially aware. Chivalry was a set of rules that they had to abide by to be true gentlemen. Just like Fred Astaire, the knights knew exactly how to dress, how to be polite to their rivals, and how to show a lady a good time."

"But I doubt they knew how to tap dance," Jessica interrupted.

He rubbed his chin thoughtfully. "You're probably right about that one. It's tough to be graceful when you're wearing a suit of armor," he mused. "Who's your favorite movie heroine?"

"I liked Scarlett O'Hara in *Gone With the Wind*. Even when things were tough for her, she always managed to pull through."

"Tough? What Scarlett went through was nothing compared to Eleanor of Aquitaine's trials. Lady Eleanor was a beautiful, resilient woman who was forced to leave her husband, her home, *and* her country. But even while she was in exile, she never gave up on the concept of courtly love." He looked up at the clock. "Am I out of time?"

Jessica, who had stopped looking at the clock a long time ago, had completely forgotten about the time. "Actually, I think you went over by about thirty seconds."

"I did?" he said, sounding disappointed.

"It doesn't matter." Jessica impulsively touched the arm of his tweed blazer. The material was softer than it looked. "Give me an example of a medieval romance."

He flashed her a brilliant smile. "So I *did* pique your interest after all!" he said triumphantly.

"I guess you did," Jessica said, shyly looking away. "But only a little," she quickly added.

48

"I bet you'll love the class once you go. In fact, I'm willing to stake a cup of coffee on it." He extended his hand. "By the way, my name is Louis."

"I'm Jessica." The touch of his hand sent shock waves through her. It took a moment for her to catch her breath. "I might just take you up on that bet," she said with a mischievous smile. "By the way—I like my coffee black."

Chapter Four

"Oooooooo! I love this song!" Denise shouted over the blaring music. She yanked Winston by the wrist and dragged him toward the dance floor.

Winston resisted. "Can't we sit this one out? My feet are killing me," he complained.

Denise, clapping in time to the music, didn't hear him or pretended not to. People moved in from all sides, and Winston realized there was no use fighting it. He was stuck.

"Come on, Winnie!" Denise shimmied up to him.

Winston laughed and twirled her in his arms. Denise pushed him away, gracefully untangling herself. When they moved too far apart, she grabbed the collar of his shirt and pulled him toward her, planting a big kiss on his lips.

Winston sighed dreamily and pinched himself to make sure it wasn't all a dream. Denise was the most beautiful, incredible woman he had ever met, and she was absolutely crazy about him. Even though they had been dating for several months, sometimes he still couldn't believe it was true. Denise was the kind of woman he used to dream about, not the kind who ever showed any interest in him. He didn't remember what life was like before Denise, and he couldn't imagine what it would be like without her. Being with Denise made Winston forget all his worries—at least for a while.

The music faded out and the DJ's voice came over the loudspeaker. "Thanks for coming out tonight. I hate to break it to you guys, but this party's over!"

Everyone groaned and the lights suddenly came on, transforming the chic dance club back into the ordinary college hall that it was before. People shuffled out, the spell broken. A few students started arguing over who would get to take the banner home. Others were standing on chairs, trying to reach the balloons that had floated to the ceiling.

"That was great!" Denise said enthusiastically, tossing a streamer around Winston's neck. "Did you have a good time?"

"Sure," Winston answered soberly. In a matter of seconds, the terrific evening had suddenly evaporated and reality hit him—hard. Winston remembered his upcoming physics test and how so far, he had done absolutely nothing to prepare for it.

"What's wrong?" Denise asked. Winston loved

the way her brow furrowed whenever she was concerned about him. "What's bugging you?"

"It's the physics exam," he confessed. "I feel guilty for not staying in and studying."

"Winnie—it's Friday night! You have the whole weekend to study." Denise pinched the tip of his nose. "You're such a worrywart."

He started to relax. "Yeah, I know. I'm supposed to meet with my study group tomorrow morning, so maybe I can get a lot of work done then." Denise was right—he *did* worry too much.

"Denise! Winston!" Anoushka Koll ran over to where they were standing. "Where are you guys headed?" she asked breathlessly.

Denise and Winston looked at each other and shrugged. "We haven't really thought about it," Denise answered.

"Well, don't even *think* about going back to our dorm," Anoushka said. "There's a huge party at Craig Maser's apartment. That's where everyone's headed right now."

Denise gave Winston's hand a squeeze. "Are you up for it, Winnie?"

He nodded. "Let's go."

As they walked out of Xavier Hall into the cool night, Winston tried not to worry about all the work that was waiting for him back in his room. There was no point in trying to study tonight. There was always tomorrow.

*   *   *

Jessica unlocked the door of room 28 in Dickenson Hall and peeked inside. The coast was clear. Elizabeth wasn't back from the party yet. Jessica smiled to herself and slipped into the room. The last thing she wanted to do was to explain where she had spent her evening.

She tossed the keys onto her desk. *I can't believe I just spent Friday night talking about medieval history in a bookstore with some guy I've never met before.* What was even weirder was that it was actually kind of fun. But she wasn't going to make a habit of it. Jessica was determined to make sure that no one found out about this strange event. Even if the word got out, it didn't matter much; her friends would never believe it.

Jessica left her clothes in a pile on the floor and slid into her favorite purple satin pajamas. It was strange how she had never seen Louis on campus before tonight, but then again he wasn't the kind of guy she would've paid much attention to. He dressed much too conservatively, and he probably spent all his time in the library. Of course, there was always the possibility that he recently transferred from another school. He seemed much more intelligent and sophisticated than most of the students at SVU. Jessica was certain that he had to be a senior.

It doesn't matter what year he is—he's definitely not your type, a little voice told her. Jessica wrapped her hair in a bun and applied a thick layer of mud mask to her face. What would happen if she bumped into him on campus? If the Thetas saw her talking to him, she'd never hear the end of it. Even though he was funny and charming, not to mention incredibly good-looking, she'd have no choice—she'd have to keep her distance. Jessica Wakefield had a reputation to uphold.

Jessica grabbed a purple hand towel and walked down the hall to the bathroom. The steaming hot water felt good as she washed off the mask. Louis was so completely different from every other man she had ever known—but maybe that wasn't such a bad thing after all. The men she had chosen in the past were totally wrong for her. Maybe she needed to branch off in a new direction. Explore uncharted territory. *Forget it. Don't waste your time*, said a voice deep inside her. *Men are all alike*.

As she patted her face dry with the towel, she looked up at her reflection in the mirror. Clever and intelligent. That's how he'd described her. What made him say that? Was that his usual pick-up line, or did he really mean it?

Jessica draped the towel over her shoulder. She reached up to take out the bun at the top of her head, but something made her pause. She stared into the mirror, lifted her chin slightly, and turned her head to the side. The bun made her look very studious, even more than Elizabeth did with her ponytail. Jessica admired her new look for a minute, then broke out in a fit of laughter. She shook the bun loose and went back to her bedroom.

*　　*　　*

Elizabeth walked through the door of the station, wearing a clean shirt and carrying the picnic basket. She had left the party early, knowing that the only way to get Tom away from his work was to show up at WSVU. Elizabeth had gone back to her dorm room to change out of the stained silk shirt and was grateful that Jessica had decided to go out after all. She wasn't in the mood to get into a fight over the shirt with her sister. Especially since her precious moments with Tom were ticking away fast.

The room was completely dark, except for the glow of the computer screen. She could tell by Tom's posture that he was completely absorbed in his work. He typed away furiously on the keyboard, as though he were about to cover an exclusive, late-breaking story of international significance.

Elizabeth put the picnic basket on the worktable. She walked over to where he was sitting and stood behind his chair. But Tom continued typing, seemingly unaware that she was even in the room. She leaned over and wrapped her arms around his shoulders.

Tom wasn't even startled. "Hi," he mumbled, his teeth clenching a pen.

Elizabeth kissed him lightly on the cheek. "How's it going?" she asked.

Tom didn't blink, his eyes still fixed on the screen. "Fine . . ." he answered distractedly.

"You're going to go blind." Elizabeth clicked

on the desk lamp. She turned around and leaned against his desk, facing him. "I just came from the party. You should have been there."

Tom scribbled in his notebook, then returned to the keyboard.

"It was wild. A herd of water buffalo crashed the party and took over the dance floor. People locked themselves in the bathrooms so they wouldn't get trampled." Elizabeth stared at him, waiting for a reaction.

"Hmmmm . . ." Tom answered.

Elizabeth sighed, blocking the computer screen with her hand. "You haven't heard a word I said, have you?"

Tom looked up at her as though he'd just woken from a deep sleep. He took the pen out of his mouth. "I'm sorry—I'm not trying to ignore you. It's just that I have so much to do before I leave."

"I know," Elizabeth said patiently. "I've come to steal you away from your work for a little while. You need a break." She showed him the picnic basket. It was filled with french bread, cheeses, strawberries, and sparkling water. "I thought maybe we could have a romantic picnic out on the quad. It's a beautiful night."

"It looks great, Liz." Tom smiled at her. "Just in time, too—I'm starved. Would you mind if we ate it here, though? I really have to finish this write-up."

Elizabeth's heart sank. "Sure. Whatever you

want," she said, her voice straining. It wasn't the moonlit rendezvous she had envisioned, but they'd have to make do. Elizabeth unfolded a checkered tablecloth and spread it out on the worktable. She filled two wineglasses with sparkling water.

Tom took a sip of the water. "This is wonderful. Thank you." He held Elizabeth by the waist and pulled her toward him.

"Anything for my star journalist," Elizabeth said proudly. She sat in his lap, her arms encircling his neck. "So what do you have left to do?"

"Everything," Tom said tiredly. "There are two pieces I have yet to finish, and I still haven't made a schedule so I can meet with the professional journalists at the conference." His face suddenly lit up. "Did I tell you that Angela Hunter is going to be there?"

"No, you didn't!" Elizabeth said with surprise. Angela Hunter was a local news anchor that Elizabeth had admired since she first became interested in journalism. "Will you have a chance to meet her?"

"I don't know." Tom ran his fingers through his hair. "On Monday morning there's supposed to be a brunch for the college journalists to mingle with the professionals. If she's there, maybe I'll try to set up a meeting with her."

Elizabeth was amazed at how cool Tom seemed about it all—as though the conference was no big deal. She would've been thrilled to have the opportunity to go to such a big event. Tom was acting like he met with award-winning journalists every day.

"What are you going to be doing while I'm away?" Tom kissed the tip of her nose.

"Other than missing you? Not much."

Tom laughed. "I mean here at the station. What do you have lined up?"

Elizabeth stood and walked over to the worktable. "Actually, I came up with an idea for a piece while I was at the party tonight. I thought I would start investigating while you were away."

Tom returned to his work. "What is it?"

Elizabeth stared at Tom while he typed. "Something interesting happened. I bumped into Gin-Yung in the bathroom, and she told me that the athletics department refused to let Todd rejoin the basketball team."

Tom frowned at the computer screen. "What's so strange about that? Todd was accepting privileges, which was highly unethical. Why should they let him back on the team?"

Elizabeth folded her arms across her chest. "You know Todd didn't act maliciously. He admitted he'd made a mistake, *and* he's paid for it."

"It doesn't matter," Tom argued. "The athletics department has no obligation to let him back on the team."

Elizabeth sank her teeth into a strawberry. "They said they would let him back on the team after the probation period. They didn't do it—I think we should find out why," she said firmly.

Tom spun his chair around and looked at her with disbelief. "Why are you so concerned about Todd? He's getting what he deserves," he said, his voice taking on a cold edge. "WSVU has wasted enough time covering the scandal. It's time to move on to something else."

Tom's words were like a pickax, chipping away at Elizabeth's confidence. It was the first time he had ever shot down one of her story ideas. "I know you don't care for Todd, but don't let that get in the way of your work. I think we need to do this piece," she said uneasily.

"This has nothing to do with how I feel about Todd," he snapped. "*I'm* the station director here, Liz, and I think it's a waste of time. End of discussion."

Elizabeth bit the insides of her cheeks, determined to hold back the tears that welled up in her eyes. Tom continued working, as if nothing had happened. She looked at the table with all the beautiful food she had gone to so much trouble to get. *What a waste of time,* she thought angrily. In a matter of minutes, the romantic evening she had hoped for had evaporated.

"I guess I'll leave you to your work," she said, quickly heading for the door before the tears started to fall.

"Elizabeth?"

Elizabeth turned around. "What?"

Tom stopped typing. His profile was illuminated

by the soft light of the computer screen. "Will I see you tomorrow before I leave?"

Elizabeth opened the door a crack, so the light from the hallway trickled in. "Maybe," she whispered as a tear rolled down her cheek.

Louis stepped out of the bookstore into the fresh night air, feeling better than he had in a long time. It was only his second day on the SVU campus, and he was already feeling at home. The students seemed very bright and much more friendly than the last school he was at. There was something comforting and safe about Sweet Valley. He hoped he would be able to stay for a long time.

Louis unlocked the door of his old silver Toyota and laid his book bag on the passenger seat. He buckled his seat belt, smiling to himself. For the first time he was actually looking forward to starting classes on Monday. Usually he was a wreck. He'd spent many sleepless nights, afraid that he'd forget his notes or his mind would suddenly go blank. But this time he was going to stay calm and take things in stride. Things were going to be different.

Louis started the car's engine and turned on the headlights. Jessica might have had something to do with his new outlook. It was an incredible coincidence that he had bumped into someone who was going to be in his seminar, especially someone as beautiful and outgoing as Jessica. From the few minutes he'd spent talking to her,

Louis sensed that they had an instant connection. During their conversation he'd felt an undercurrent, an energy in which they'd seemed to understand each other on a deeper level than most people did. But what he'd liked most about her was the spark that lit up her eyes. In her there was a fiery passion for life—something he had lost.

Louis sighed contentedly. The headlights of his car sliced through the darkness as he drove down the long road toward the edge of campus. It was going to be a busy weekend, but he liked it that way. There was still so much to do before Monday. There were lesson plans to make, policies to learn. He still had to set up his desk in the office he would have to share with Professor Stark. It was only a temporary placement, until the renovations were finished. Then he'd have his own office in the history department.

Louis imagined how wonderful it would be to finally have his own office. He knew exactly how he'd decorate it. He envisioned dark, solid wood bookshelves holding volumes of his favorite works. He'd bring in brass reading lamps and a red leather chair. The walls would be decorated with medieval prints, and maybe even an antique wall tapestry if he could find one cheap enough. Then, of course, was the finishing touch. Something he had bought some time ago, waiting for the perfect place to use it—and Sweet Valley seemed to be the perfect place. It was a brass door plaque with his name engraved on it. A smile crossed Louis's lips as he pictured it bolted to his office door. *Professor Louis Miles—Medieval History.*

Chapter Five

Winston buried his face in the pillow to block the bright rays of sunlight that streamed through the window blinds. His head felt a little achy, like it usually did when he stayed out too late. His brain was too clouded to remember what time he had come back to his room. All he could recall was that he and Denise had walked back across campus together, hand in hand. It had to have been close to dawn, since a thin line of orange had started to appear over the horizon. The only image that burned clear in his mind was how great Denise had looked in the soft light.

Covering his eyes with one hand, Winston reached up to adjust the blinds. He sank back into the comfort of his bed, grateful that the alarm hadn't sounded yet. At least he had a little more time to sleep before he had to meet with his study group.

Winston lazily rolled over to glance at the time. He looked at the clock, then rubbed his eyes and looked at it again. It was noon.

This can't be right! Winston thought as he bolted upright. He looked at the clock again. He had forgotten to set the alarm. The study group was supposed to meet two hours ago. With any luck, they were still at the library, working on the physics problems.

A shot of adrenaline rushed through his body, and Winston was fully awake. He raced to his closet and pulled on a pair of jeans and an old T-shirt. Winston squirted a gob of gel into his hands and ran his fingers through his hair. He accidentally put on too much, making his head look like it had just collided with an oil tanker. Winston made a face as he wiped his gelled fingers on the front of his jeans. Maybe they wouldn't notice.

"How could I be so stupid?" he asked himself as he jogged down the path toward the library. "How could I forget to set my alarm clock?" Before he could come up with a good excuse, his father's voice rang clearly in the back of his head. *The alarm clock had nothing to do with it, Winston. You shouldn't have stayed out all night.*

"What was I supposed to do?" Winston argued with the voice inside his head. Denise was having fun and he didn't want to ruin it. How could he say no to the woman he was crazy about? Didn't his father understand love?

Winston opened the door to the library. He

compulsively touched the top of his head. Even though he ran all the way, his hair hadn't moved at all. Winston skipped down the stairs to the lower level. The study group was supposed to meet near the periodicals. He slowed down his walk and tried to catch his breath. He wanted to seem casual.

What will they say when they see me? Winston wondered self-consciously. He hated the thought of everyone stopping what they were doing to stare at him. Was there any way to sneak into a group meeting two hours late and not be noticed?

He decided he'd have to make up some sort of excuse so he wouldn't seem like a total jerk. *I'll tell them the power went out in my dorm.* No, that wouldn't work—some of the people in the group lived in his dorm. Maybe he could tell them he was late because he was so engrossed in a physics problem he lost track of time. But that excuse had way too much backfire potential. They'd probably want to look at the problem he was working on. Then he'd be in serious trouble.

He turned the corner next to the newspaper shelves for the third time. *Where are they?* He'd already made three circles around the room, and the group was nowhere in sight. Winston slumped into a chair and set his books on the table in front of him. He had missed the meeting.

Winston laid his head on the tabletop, wondering what to do next. His eyes were heavy and his head pounded. How was he supposed to get his homework done now? There was no way he'd be able to finish it all by himself. He was so far behind in his work that he didn't even know where to begin. Winston closed his eyes and took a deep breath, waiting for the pain in his chest to subside.

"I'm sorry I missed the party last night," Nina said, her braids clicking as she plopped down onto her bed. "I fell asleep on my books in the library."

"Sounds like you had more fun than I did," Elizabeth answered dryly. Last night after she'd visited Tom, she went back to her room and tried to fall asleep. She'd tossed and turned, replaying their argument again and again in her mind. She had finally come to the conclusion that maybe she'd overreacted a bit. But still, Tom had been so insensitive, and that's what bothered her most. What had come over him? Was it just a mood he was in, or was she getting to know a side of Tom she had never seen before?

"Pretzel?" Nina passed the bag to Elizabeth. "They're fat-free."

Elizabeth made a face. "No thanks." She wasn't hungry.

Nina took a handful out of the bag. "You're missing out—these are really good. I think I'm getting addicted to them."

Elizabeth's eyes were fixed on the Lenny Kravitz poster that was hanging on Nina's closet door. A tiny chill ran down her back. She hugged her knees to stay warm.

Nina looked at the poster and then at Elizabeth. "Okay, Liz—time to fess up. What's going on in that head of yours?"

"Is it that obvious?" she asked, coming out of the daze.

"Completely. I know you're not *that* big a fan of Lenny." Nina bit into a pretzel. "What happened to put you in such a funk?"

Elizabeth looked at Nina. "I don't know," she said, leaning back against Nina's multistriped pillows. "I guess it has to do with Tom."

Nina nodded knowingly. "You're upset because he's going to Las Vegas," she said in between bites of her pretzels. "To be honest, I have no idea how the most romantic couple at SVU will survive the separation—you're practically joined at the hip."

Elizabeth frowned. "Maybe we were at one time, but things seem different lately. Tom's acting weird."

"Like how?" Nina asked.

Elizabeth gazed absently out the window. "Well, for one thing, when I went to see him at the station last night, I brought a picnic basket for us to share. I was hoping we could have a romantic picnic on the quad. I wanted everything to be perfect." There was a sinking feeling in the pit of her stomach. "But he wanted to have it at the station, so he could keep working. He totally took me for granted."

Nina handed Elizabeth her favorite teddy bear. It had white fur and a big red bow tied around its neck. "I'm sure it has nothing to do with you, Liz. It's the conference. Tom's had a lot on his mind, and you've said yourself that he's been stressed out about it." Nina took another bite of pretzel. "Tom loves you. Things will get back to normal as soon as the conference is over."

Elizabeth held the teddy bear close to her. Its soft fur was warm and comforting. "I hope so," she answered. She wanted to believe that all their problems were because of the conference, but Elizabeth had a gut feeling that maybe there was something more. Something had changed in the way they worked together that was starting to affect their love relationship. Ever since Tom had been invited to the conference, he was no longer treating her as an equal at the station. Instead, she was made to feel like a rookie.

"And he did something else last night that really bugged me," Elizabeth said, playing with the ends of the bear's satin bow.

Nina tucked her legs under her. "Oh, yeah? What'd he do?"

"I had an idea for a story, and he shot it down immediately. He's never done that before. We've always been a team." Tears of frustration came to her eyes just thinking about it. "I don't get it."

Nina's eyes narrowed thoughtfully. "I think I do. Promise you won't get upset at what I'm about to say?"

Elizabeth looked at her curiously. "Promise."

A look of diplomacy came over Nina's face. "I

think the problem is that you two are being competitive with each other."

Elizabeth's eyebrows arched in surprise. "What do you mean?" she asked.

Nina paused. "Well, both of you are great journalists, and you've always worked great together. So when one of you gets special recognition, the other one feels left out."

"Meaning me . . ." Elizabeth answered slowly.

"Exactly. But Tom has been at WSVU longer than you have. Even though he is the station manager, I think that maybe you're having a hard time taking orders from him." Nina touched Elizabeth's arm lightly. "I hope you don't mind me saying that."

"No—it's all right," Elizabeth said honestly. Nina was her closest friend, and she always valued her opinion. "Actually, I think you may be right." She and Tom had been working as a team for so long that she had never really thought of him as a competitor before. Suddenly they were being separated, and things were different. "It makes a lot of sense."

Nina tucked a stray braid behind her ear. She sat upright, seeming more confident in her analysis. "Tom might be feeling a little awkward about it too. That could be why he's acting so strange."

Elizabeth felt a tiny rumble in her stomach, and she reached for the pretzel bag. Everything Nina said seemed so logical. Now that she knew what the problem was, they could work on a solution. Elizabeth flashed her friend a smile. "Have you ever considered being a psychologist?"

Nina smiled back. "Actually, I forgot to tell you—I *am* a psychologist." She held out her open palm. "By the way, that will be fifty bucks."

Elizabeth slapped her hand and laughed. "I'd better get out of here before this starts costing me more money." She slipped her feet into her leather flats and grabbed a handful of pretzels.

"Where are you going?" Nina asked as she licked the traces of salt from her fingertips.

Elizabeth tossed Nina the teddy bear. "Tom's flight leaves in just a few hours. I want to clear the air before he goes."

"That's my girl," Nina said proudly. "You let that boy know exactly what he's going to be missing."

Elizabeth flashed her a sly smile. "Don't worry. I will."

"Just think! No more disgusting cafeteria food!" Lila exclaimed as she tossed a limp french fry onto Jessica's plate. "Pretty soon it's going to be filet mignon every single night!"

Jessica rolled her eyes. She flicked the greasy fry off her tray onto the cafeteria table. "Who's going to do the dishes?"

"Bruce will," Lila answered thoughtfully. "Better yet—we'll buy a dishwasher!"

Jessica debated whether or not to get a bowl of frozen yogurt, but the line was getting too long. "Why don't you just hire a cleaning staff while you're at it?" she said dryly.

A look of triumph crossed Lila's elegant face. "We're already a step ahead of you, Jess. Bruce has arranged to have a maid come in twice a week."

Jessica had to hand it to Lila: whenever she got an idea in her head, she took it as far as it could possibly go. Unfortunately Lila's sense of reality usually ended up getting lost somewhere along the way. Jessica bit into her chicken salad sandwich. "So where is this love nest going to be?"

Lila pushed aside her tray and examined her polished nails. "Good question. We definitely want a place that's close to the beach and not too far from school. We're supposed to go looking with a real-estate agent on Monday. Do you want to come?"

"No thanks," Jessica said. She had been on countless shopping trips with Lila and knew what torture it could be. It took Lila hours on end just to pick out the right shade of lipstick. Jessica couldn't imagine how long it would take her to find the perfect apartment. "Tell you what, though—I'll stop by once you have the place picked out."

"Suit yourself," Lila said unflinchingly. She stared out the window with a silly smile glued to her face. A small robin landed on the windowsill and Lila pointed to it, squealing with delight. "Look at that little bird! He's soooo cute!" she said in a baby voice.

Jessica's upper lip curled into a sneer. *People in love are absolutely nauseating,* she thought. Love could turn an otherwise normal person into a babbling idiot. Just the fact that sophisticated Lila Fowler was sitting in the middle of the SVU cafeteria making cooing noises to some random bird was enough evidence to support her theory.

"How's Prince Charming?" Jessica asked, her voice touched with sarcasm.

Lila's face took on a dreamy expression. "Wonderful. He's perfect, Jess. I can't wait until we move in together. We're going to have so much fun."

"Oh, it's going to be fun, all right. Just wait until you have to pick up his smelly socks." Jessica wrinkled her nose in disgust. "Nothing kills romance faster than dirty laundry."

Lila pursed her lips and gave her chestnut brown hair a quick toss over her shoulder. "First of all, Bruce's laundry doesn't stink, and second of all, we'll have a maid to do the wash," she said in a firm tone. "Why are you trying so hard to burst my bubble?"

Jessica almost choked on her mouthful of food. Did Lila really think that Bruce's socks smelled like roses? Jessica's mouth contorted as she tried to contain her laughter. Maybe she was being a little harsh on Lila, though. This was an exciting time for her. But Jessica couldn't help being negative. She had lived through all of this before. "I didn't mean to spoil it for you, Li. It's just that living with someone is a huge step. I should know—I've been there. Sometimes romance isn't all it's cracked up to be."

"Don't be such a wet blanket," Lila pouted. She took a sip from her bottle of mineral water. "What Bruce and I have is completely different from what went on with you and Mike. You have no idea what I'm going through."

Jessica's heart ached at the sound of Mike's name. It was true, he was nothing like the egomaniac that Lila was obsessed with. Still, Jessica couldn't imagine that their relationships were that different. She had been madly in love with Mike, just as Lila was with Bruce. She knew what it was like to want to do everything with the person you loved. But Jessica had learned that spending every possible moment with that person meant making sacrifices and compromises. Living with someone meant trying to tolerate their faults and weaknesses. Sometimes it was simply too much to ask for.

Jessica looked directly into Lila's eyes. "All I'm saying is that it's a big commitment and responsibility."

Lila threw her a haughty look. "Excuse me, Jess, but you're starting to sound like your drippy sister Elizabeth."

Jessica frowned. "That's not nice, Li. No one can call Elizabeth a drip but me." A tingling panic suddenly gripped her. "Do I really sound like Elizabeth?"

Lila gave her a solemn nod. "Totally."

Jessica's brow furrowed. It was bad enough that she'd hung out last night in a bookstore and actually enjoyed it. Now she was starting to sound

72

like Elizabeth. The last thing Jessica wanted was to be as boring and conservative as her sister.

Lila gave Jessica a wink. "Speaking of Elizabeth, I saw her last night at the party but I didn't see you anywhere. Did you have a hot date last night?"

Jessica stiffened. *What am I going to tell her?* She couldn't say that she'd spent Friday night in a bookstore talking to some guy about medieval history. Lila would probably tell one of the Thetas, and the next thing Jessica knew, it'd be all over the sorority. Her reputation would be shattered. "I didn't do anything," she answered brusquely. "I just hung out in my room."

Lila shot her a sly smile. "You're not fooling anyone, Wakefield. Come on, you can tell me. Who is he?"

Jessica shrugged. "There's nothing to tell," she said. A picture of Louis's handsome face and piercing green eyes flashed through Jessica's mind, causing her to tremble. She quickly pushed the image of Louis out of her head. "I'm through with love," she said confidently, even though her body was still trembling.

"Don't forget to make a schedule so someone is around to answer the station phones every night," Tom said distractedly as he stuffed WSVU story write-ups into manila folders. Videotapes and their plastic cases were strewn all over the office. "It's crucial that someone is always by the phones in case an important story breaks."

"Got it." Elizabeth jotted down notes on her pocket calendar as she followed Tom around the station. He was rushing around haphazardly, trying to clean up the office and spouting off directions at the same time. Elizabeth could hardly keep up.

He stopped suddenly, and Elizabeth almost bumped into him. "I've already handed out assignments to the writers, and it should be enough while I'm away." He scratched his chin thoughtfully. "If it isn't, go to the story-idea file. It's in the corner over—"

"Tom, I know where it is," Elizabeth said patiently. "I work here, remember?"

"I'm just making sure, that's all." Tom turned suddenly, and Elizabeth jumped to the side just as he plowed past her. "One more thing. Make sure someone puts in a data tape—"

"To back up the hard drive," Elizabeth finished. She sat down on a metal stool in a corner of the room, safely out of Tom's way. "You're acting like a nervous parent. You may find it hard to believe, Mr. Watts, but this station will be just fine without you," she said teasingly.

Tom shoved some papers into his carry-on bag. "I know everything will be fine. The station's in good hands." He stopped for a moment, his face suddenly lighting up. "I almost forgot to tell you—Craig Maser's coach got a call yesterday from Angela Hunter. She wants to do an interview with Craig before the fight, and yours truly will be able to sit in on the interview."

Elizabeth's eyes gleamed. "Tom, that's great," she said brightly. "You'll have to call and tell me all about it."

Tom started putting the videotapes back into their cases. "Which reminds me—I'm going to call you once or twice to make sure that everything is running smoothly. The problem is, I don't know when. The schedule is going to be so hectic."

"That's okay," Elizabeth answered. A feeling of disappointment fluttered inside her. She had hoped he'd make an attempt to call more often, and that it wouldn't be just for business. This was going to be the longest they'd ever been apart. Elizabeth could feel a tiny hole in her chest, and it opened wider with every thought of them being apart. Tom hadn't even stepped on the plane yet and she was missing him already.

Tom placed the last video on the shelf and took a seat next to Elizabeth. "What story were you planning to work on this week?" he asked. Elizabeth noticed that Tom's facial expression was the same as it always was, as if this were any other normal day. Didn't he have the same sense of loss that she was beginning to feel? Was he going to miss her?

Elizabeth stared deeply into his eyes, wanting desperately to see what was going on behind them. She set her calendar down on the table beside them. "You know I had originally planned to investigate the reasons why Todd is being left off the team. But I've given it a lot of thought, and I've come to the conclusion that you were right. There's nothing more to look into."

Tom gently caressed her hand. "I'm glad you agree," he said, sounding relieved. "I didn't mean to sound so harsh last night. I've just had a lot on my mind lately."

Elizabeth's lips curved into a smile. Tom was sounding more like his old self. Soon everything would be back to normal, just like Nina said. "I understand," she answered, covering his hand with her own. "That's why I thought I'd explore the issue from another angle."

Tom pulled back. "What do you mean?"

Elizabeth brushed the hair out of her eyes. "Well, I thought I could turn it into a human-interest story. Maybe I could approach it strictly from Todd's point of view, and how all this has affected him."

Tom shook his head. His jaw tensed, as if he were gritting his teeth. "Why do you keep insisting on writing about Todd?" he demanded.

Elizabeth looked at him strangely. "I'm not insisting on anything," she said. "It just seems to me that there's a story in what's been happening to him."

"No way." Tom's voice took on a jealous edge. His eyes hardened. "Poor old Todd has already had too much airtime at WSVU," he said bitingly.

Elizabeth folded her arms across her chest defensively. There was no point in arguing her case any further. Tom's mind was already made up.

Tom sat in silence, rubbing his face with his hands. Suddenly he stood up. "I've got something you should work on," he said. Tom walked over to stack of cardboard boxes in the corner of the room. They were old and torn and covered with dirt. "The piece about alumni donations. The dean's been after me to do a story because SVU hasn't received a large alumni donation in five years." He blew off the tops of the boxes, creating a cloud of dust. "You can start by going through these old files."

Elizabeth protested. "But that was *your* piece—"

"And now it's yours," Tom said flatly. "I'm sorry, but I was too busy getting ready for the conference. I didn't have enough time to get everything done."

"So you're giving it to me."

"I can't do it all, Elizabeth," he said coolly, shrugging.

Elizabeth's cheeks were flushed with anger. "Don't expect me to do your work just because *you* couldn't get it done in time!"

"Look, the alumni piece didn't have priority— it could wait," Tom argued, raising his voice.

"You mean it could wait until it could be conveniently passed on to another journalist!" Elizabeth's temper flared. The floodgates were open, words spilling out of her before she could stop them. "Is it because you think you're too good to work on such a dull story?"

A heavy silence hung in the air. Elizabeth bit her lip, instantly wishing she could take back what she had just said.

Tom turned away from her. Without saying a word, he picked up the stack of folders and started putting them back into the dusty boxes. "You know, Liz," he said after a few moments. His voice started to crack. "I thought you'd be happy for me. This conference could be a big break for my career."

"I *am* happy for you, Tom. I really am," Elizabeth said, nearly pleading. *How did things get out of hand so fast?* she wondered. One minute they were talking about the station, the next they were ready to tear each other's eyes out. She swallowed hard, trying to get rid of the lump that was wedged in her throat. "I just wish you wouldn't order me around like a child."

Tom looked long and hard at Elizabeth, as if she were a stranger he knew he had met sometime before. "Running WSVU is my job. You may not like the decisions I make, but I'm just doing what I think is best for the station."

Elizabeth blinked back a tear. "How about doing what's best for us?"

Tom looked away, his face stony and silent. He stuffed a few folders into his bag and turned off his computer. "My plane leaves in two hours," he said quietly as he slung the bag over his shoulder. "I have to go pack."

Don't let him leave without making up, a little

voice inside Elizabeth's head told her. But she stood frozen in place as she watched him slowly walk out the door. She felt as if a thick glass wall had suddenly been put between them, and there was nothing she could say that would reach Tom.

Chapter Six

There should be a law against classes this early in the morning, Jessica thought sleepily as she wandered into the lecture hall. The hall was nearly empty except for a few groggy students munching on bagels and sipping cups of black coffee. Apparently she wasn't the only one who was having trouble waking up.

Jessica slumped into a hard wooden chair in the middle of the room. The walls were bare and unremarkable, except for a few maps and an enormous chalkboard at the front of the room. There was an old wooden desk and a metal folding chair for the professor in the front. The overhead lights hadn't been turned on yet, and the only light source came from two dingy windows that looked out at the brick wall of a nearby building. With nothing to look at and no one to talk to, Jessica figured she'd be asleep in ten minutes.

Isabella doesn't know how lucky she is, Jessica mused. The film class met in the evenings, in the video screening room in the library. Jessica had been there before for other classes. The chairs were cloth covered and comfortable, not like the hard wooden ones that were in every other classroom. An added bonus was that it was too dark to take notes. The only thing to do was sit back, relax, and enjoy a great movie.

"I wonder what Louis would say to that," Jessica whispered to herself as she searched her bag for a notebook and pen. She smiled when she thought of Louis flipping through the gigantic Medieval History textbook and how excited he was by this incredibly boring subject. It was funny how he'd managed to get her interested too, even if it was only for about five minutes.

There was something about Louis, something she couldn't quite put her finger on, that fascinated her. It was more than just his gorgeous looks—it was a confidence and a passion she hadn't seen in many other people. Jessica was certain he could make even nuclear physics sound interesting.

A few students strolled in one by one, dressed in sweats and looking like they'd just fallen out of bed. From the pained expressions on their faces, Jessica could tell that Medieval History wasn't their first choice either.

She watched the door, waiting for Louis to enter. He had to be in this class, with his insatiable interest in the subject. *What would he be wearing?* she wondered. In a sleepy haze, she had only managed a pair of old jeans over a white bodysuit. She couldn't imagine that he'd be awake enough to be dressed up the way she'd seen him in the bookstore, with a tweed jacket and loafers. But somehow she couldn't picture him wearing anything else.

Jessica slid her bag onto the empty seat next to her. She secretly hoped that Louis would come in late, when all the seats were taken, so he'd have to sit next to her. If all else failed, at least he could keep her awake during the boring lecture.

The room was abuzz with conversation as students continued to stream in. It was only a few minutes before the class was supposed to begin, and there was still no sign of a professor. A few people stood around waiting, wondering if he would show up at all.

If he doesn't show in five minutes, I'm going back to bed. Jessica yawned. She was already thinking about how great it would be to slide under the warm covers. She slouched down in her seat, resting her head against the stiff back of the chair.

Suddenly Louis came flying through the door.

Jessica bolted upright when she saw him. His hair was slightly windblown and he was wearing the same tweed jacket he'd worn on Friday night, but this time he was wearing a dress shirt and necktie. Jessica removed her bag from the seat next to her and waved at him, pointing to the empty seat.

Louis smiled warmly and waved back, then turned around and headed to the front of the classroom. *Where is he going?* Jessica wondered. She sank back in her seat. *I should've known,* she thought dryly. He was definitely the type to sit at the front of the class.

Louis walked up to the professor's desk and laid a briefcase on the desktop. Jessica watched in puzzlement as he took a few books out of the case and put them on the table. He was probably a teaching assistant, Jessica reasoned. Definitely a good person to know. She stared at him, watching every careful move as he emptied the contents of the briefcase onto the desk. He wasn't kidding when he said he liked medieval history. It was his life.

Louis walked around to the front of the desk and leaned against it. He held up his hands. "Quiet, please," he said above the noise in the room. Students scattered, filling in the remaining seats.

"I'm glad to see that you all managed to drag yourselves out of bed this morning," Louis said jokingly. "Welcome to A Seminar on Medieval History." He turned and started to write on the chalkboard. "For those of you who don't know me, my name is Professor Louis Miles."

"Do you have a moment, sir?" Winston asked as he knocked on the doorframe of the office that Professor Stark and Professor Miles shared.

Professor Stark looked up from the problem

sets he was correcting. His thinning hair was steely gray, and he wore a navy blue bow tie with matching suspenders. "Come on in, Mr. Egbert," he said coolly. "I've been expecting you."

"You have?" Winston eyes widened. *How did he know I was coming?* he wondered nervously. Winston looked for a place to sit but the entire office, including the chairs, was cluttered with cardboard boxes. Professor Miles's desk was pushed against the opposite wall, and a low office divider cut the room in half.

"I'll be glad when these renovations are finished," Professor Stark grumbled to no one in particular. He lifted a box that was on the chair next to his desk and motioned for Winston to sit down. Then he turned to Professor Miles, who was seated at his desk on the other side of the divider. "Louis, you don't mind if I put this on your side of the room for a few minutes, do you?"

"No, not at all," he answered good-naturedly. "We don't have a lot of room to work with." Louis sounded so easygoing that Winston wished he were his professor instead of old Stark.

Professor Stark looked down his nose at Winston. "Due to the construction that's going on all over campus, Professor Miles and I are forced to share an office. If you wish to speak to me in private, we can go elsewhere."

"No—this is fine." Winston sat down in the chair and took a deep breath. He tried not to stare at the bushy gray eyebrows that were casting shadows over Stark's eyes. "I just wanted to tell you that I'm still working on the problem set, and I'll be able to give it to you at the beginning of the next class."

Professor Stark pinched his lips thoughtfully. "The problem set was due today, Mr. Egbert."

"I—I know." Winston shifted in his chair. "It's just that I'm having some difficulty with them. I need a little more time." He looked away and focused his attention on the autographed photo of Albert Einstein hanging over the professor's desk.

"You had all weekend," Stark answered without a hint of sympathy. "You had plenty of time."

Winston suddenly felt as if someone had turned up the heat in the room about twenty degrees. Color flooded his face and beads of perspiration appeared on his forehead. His mind went blank. "Physics is a tough subject for me. . . . I'm not doing very well, as you already know. I was hoping you could give me some extra problems to do. You know, extra-credit work to help me out."

Professor Stark lowered his head and peered at Winston over the top of his reading glasses. He stared at him without blinking, saying nothing for several uncomfortable seconds. The professor's gray eyes were boring holes right through Winston to the back of his brain. "Mr. Egbert," he said solemnly. "Why should I give you more problems to do when you don't even turn in the ones that were assigned to begin with? Frankly, I don't believe the material is too hard for you to grasp. The real problem is that you're not taking the time to learn it."

Winston sat in silence, not even moving to brush away the drop of sweat that was running down his nose. How could he plead his case when deep down, he knew that the professor was right?

Stark cleared his throat with authority. "Right now, you are in danger of not passing my course. I don't need to tell you that failure will mean you will have to take another science class in order to fulfill your graduation requirements. It's safe to say that you will not be majoring in any of the pure sciences?"

"Correct, sir."

"At this point, your only hope is to do extremely well on the next two exams—the first of which is coming up in a week."

Winston couldn't contain his surprise. "A week? I thought it was two weeks away!" he blurted. It would be hard enough to pass the test with only two weeks to study. One week would be impossible.

"You were mistaken," the professor answered. "If you had paid attention in class, you would have known that I had to move the test up a week."

Winston's face turned a darker shade of red. A sharp tingle of panic slowly crawled down his spine as Winston came to a horrifying realization. He was in deep trouble.

*   *   *

Jessica leaned against the wall just outside the office that Professor Stark and Professor Miles shared. Standing in the hallway, she heard fragments of a conference going on between Winston Egbert and Professor Stark. She couldn't really hear what they were saying, but Jessica sensed by the professor's tone that things weren't going too well for Winston.

The cup of coffee in her hand started to burn her fingers, so Jessica set it on the bench next to the door. She craned her neck, peeking around the corner into the office. From the angle she was at she caught a glimpse of Louis, bent over his desk. He was writing something down on a yellow notepad. Jessica wished she could tiptoe in and tap him on the shoulder to get his attention, but she was afraid to interrupt the meeting, even though she had a feeling that Winston would've liked her to.

How am I going to get his attention? There was little she could do without causing a disturbance. She thought of shooting a paper airplane, but decided on mental telepathy instead. She stared intently at the back of his head. *Look over here, Louis.* Jessica concentrated, focusing all her energy on him. She gasped when a moment later, he looked up from his work and glanced over his shoulder. He smiled when he saw her.

Jessica waved, mouthing the word "Hi." She lifted the cup of coffee in the air for him to see. He dropped whatever it was that he was doing and came out into the hallway.

"Don't tell me you came to pay your debts," he whispered, pointing to the cup.

"You won the bet," Jessica said, handing him the cup. She couldn't help noticing the way the flecks of green in his necktie brought out the color of his eyes. "With cream and sugar, just the way you like it."

"Thank you." Louis took a sip of the coffee. His facial features seemed more chiseled, more defined than she remembered. "Does this mean you're staying in the class?"

"As a matter of fact, it does." Jessica reached into her handbag and handed him a slip. "I just need you to sign this, and it'll be official."

He took a silver pen out of his blazer pocket and signed the paper with a triumphant flourish. "You've made a wise decision, Jessica." He beamed. "I'm glad to have you in my class. Medieval history is a fascinating subject."

"So I've been told," Jessica answered, flashing him a one-hundred-megawatt smile. She walked over to the water fountain at the other side of the hall. "You're a good spokesman for the subject. Have you ever considered becoming a professor?"

Louis laughed and followed Jessica to the fountain. "I probably should have told you—but you did the best double take I've ever seen."

Louis's laughter was light and easy, like a glider coasting through the atmosphere. Jessica felt as though she were joking around with an old friend instead of a professor she had met only a few days before. She had forgotten how easy he was to talk to—how comfortable he made her feel. "So how shocked did I look, Professor? Did my jaw drop?" Jessica pulled back her hair and leaned over to take a drink from the water fountain.

"No, nothing that severe," he said. Jessica could feel his eyes on her as he spoke. "But you did look stunned for at least a half hour."

As she drank the water, Jessica lowered her head. A golden strand of hair escaped her grasp, cascading toward the stream of water. Louis reached out and gently tucked the strand of hair behind her ear. His fingers grazed her earlobe and seemed to linger there for a moment before moving away from her.

Jessica stood up slowly, letting her hair fall around her shoulders. She lowered her eyes at first, feeling too shy to look at him as she wiped a few drops of water from her lips. Her gaze was drawn upward, following the length of his neck, tracing the strong line of his jaw to his face. She looked up to see his beautiful green eyes staring right back at her.

Louis stared at Jessica, taken aback by what he had just done. *Was that inappropriate?* He hadn't had time to think—only to react. A strand of her hair had fallen, and he had reached out instinctively. He hadn't given it a second thought; touching her seemed so natural. He could still feel the silky texture of her hair on his fingertips.

She was staring at him. "So I'll see you in class?" he said in his most professional voice. He hoped his spontaneous gesture didn't offend Jessica. The last thing he wanted was to upset her. He handed her the signed slip.

"I'll be there," she said, taking the slip from him. As she grabbed the piece of paper, their hands touched for the briefest moment. In that second Louis felt a surge of energy rush through his fingers to the rest of his body. Jessica slowly turned and walked away down the long corridor. Louis watched until she was no longer in sight. He took a sip of his coffee and went back inside his office.

Chapter Seven

"Take a left at the next light," said Marilyn Parker, the real-estate agent, as she directed Bruce from the backseat of his Jeep Cherokee. Bruce paused in the middle of the intersection to let a long line of oncoming cars pass. When it was completely clear, he slowly turned the corner.

Hurry up! Lila thought impatiently. *I bet a golf cart could go faster than this.* So what if Bruce wanted to be careful not to damage his brand-new Jeep. As far as she was concerned, he was overdoing it. There was no excuse for driving ten miles per hour. Besides, she was dying to see their new apartment.

"I think you'll really like this place," Mrs. Parker said enthusiastically. Lila noticed that her thin lips would have benefited greatly from a little lip liner. "It's close to the beach, and I think it will suit your needs perfectly."

Lila looked at Bruce and smiled. He squeezed her hand. Lila had a nervous, fluttering sensation in her stomach. It was almost too good to be true. In a few moments they were about to see their new home.

"Keep going to the end," the agent chimed. They drove through the narrow roads lined with trees and pretty beach houses. Lila rolled down her window and smelled the clean ocean air. Sweet Valley University felt a million miles away.

Maybe the real-estate agent will let us spend the night here, Lila hoped. She wasn't ready to go back to reality yet. The beach was already calling to her, and she had just bought four new bikinis for the occasion. Bruce's eyes were going to pop right out of their sockets.

"And we're here," Mrs. Parker said brightly. Bruce reached the dead end and turned into a driveway with a FOR RENT sign posted. Lila took off her sunglasses to get a better look. Standing in front of them was an enormous beach house that was two stories tall. It was very modern and light, with large glass windows around the perimeter. From the driveway they could see the stone fireplace in the living room. Beyond that, they could see through to the glass doors at the front of the house, which opened onto a patio with a pool. At the top of the building was a balcony, overlooking the ocean. Lila was in heaven.

"Oh, Bruce," she gushed excitedly. "It's absolutely perfect."

The agent cleared her throat and gave Bruce a quick tap on the shoulder. "Excuse me," she said uncomfortably. "This isn't the right one. Your apartment is across the street."

Lila looked in her rearview mirror. Directly behind them was another driveway with a FOR RENT sign posted on the edge of a weedy lawn. The building was about one quarter the size of the one in front of them. It was covered in drab gray shingles, many of which had fallen off. From the outside, it looked as though there couldn't be more than four rooms in the whole place. Bruce carefully backed the Jeep into the driveway across the street, and Lila cringed as the house loomed closer and closer in her rearview mirror.

Mrs. Parker got out first, smoothing the wrinkles of her plum business suit. "I know it needs a little work, but trust me—it's the perfect place for a couple just starting out."

Both Bruce and Lila hadn't budged an inch. The agent looked at them pleadingly through the Jeep window. Lila couldn't even move to unbuckle her seat belt. She looked at Bruce. His fingers gripped the ignition key, but he still hadn't turned off the motor.

"I guess we could at least take a look," he said to Lila. "It can't hurt."

Lila stuck out her bottom lip, then stepped out of the Jeep. Mrs. Parker consolingly put her arm around her. "Give it a chance, honey," she whispered in her ear. "You'll love it. It has lots of character." The agent rushed ahead, keys in hand. "Your apartment is on the top floor."

Top floor? Lila shot Bruce a look of horror as she followed the agent around to the back of the building. It certainly didn't look like this place had more than one floor. In fact, Lila was certain that the upstairs apartment couldn't be much more than an attic.

"What's nice about this place is that you have your own entrance." Mrs. Parker smiled as she cautiously walked up the rickety wooden steps in her high heels. "It's very private."

Bruce leaned over and whispered in Lila's ear, "It's very private except for the fact that your neighbors can hear the boards creaking under your feet every time you go up and down the stairs." Lila suppressed her sudden urge to giggle. Even when things looked grim, Bruce always knew how to make her laugh.

The agent unlocked the door. "This is a very affordable efficiency apartment. With a few personal touches, it can be quite cozy."

They walked into the main room. The first thing Lila noticed was the dingy yellow paint. The walls followed the shape of the roof—slanting like a triangle, meeting at a point directly over their heads. Lila figured she'd be able to touch the peak if she stretched on her tiptoes, but she had no desire to come in contact with anything in the apartment.

"Watch your head, Bruce," Mrs. Parker said with a smile. "I realize this is an unusual shape—it may take a little getting used to." Bruce nodded from the doorway, his muscular neck and shoulders curved so that he wouldn't hit the top of the doorframe.

Mrs. Parker held her arms up high in the air, as if she were showing the presidential suite of a four-star hotel. "This is your main living area and kitchen."

Lila stood in place, careful not to touch anything. Against the wall to her right was an old-fashioned pea green stove and matching refrigerator. In between the two appliances was a deep porcelain sink, stained with rust. Instead of cabinets, there were a few open shelves already filled with pots and pans.

"Over here is your breakfast nook."

The nook Mrs. Parker was speaking of was a small wooden table and two chairs. There were a few dried-up crumbs on the tabletop, left over, Lila assumed, from the last unfortunate tenants. Only a few feet away, on the other side of the room, was a couch, an armchair, and a coffee table. One of the legs of the coffee table was shorter than the others, and it was propped up with a thick book.

"Of course it comes fully furnished."

Lila stared down at the brown plaid upholstery. Her stomach was churning. "I see," she said with distaste.

Bruce was still huddled in the doorway. He seemed to have no intention of moving any farther inside. Lila pointed to a brass rod and pink plastic curtain on the opposite side of the room. "What's behind that?" she asked.

Mrs. Parker laughed in a way that reminded Lila of fingernails scraping against a chalkboard. "It's quite ingenious, really," the agent said, walking the few steps to the other side of the room. "It's a terrific space saver." She yanked back the curtain.

Lila gasped.

"Why is there a bathtub in the kitchen?" Bruce asked.

"It's not just a bath but a shower, too." The agent fiddled with the knobs. Brown, rusty water spurted out of the showerhead. Lila turned away in fright. "I can't believe it, Bruce. This is horrible!" she hissed under her breath.

"Shall we see the rest of the place?" Mrs. Parker's cheeriness was starting to grate on Lila's nerves. "Come on, you two. Don't judge the place until you've seen everything," she coaxed.

Lila and Bruce marched sullenly down the dark, narrow hallway. "This is your bathroom." The agent pointed to a tiny, dark closet with a toilet. "The light in there is broken, but I'm sure your landlord could have it fixed before you move in." She walked on into the bedroom. "Watch your—"

"OUCH!" Bruce had forgotten for a moment that the ceiling was low and accidentally rammed his head into the doorway.

"—head." The agent laughed nervously. "As I

said before, it will take some getting used to. . . ." She moved into the room, making grand gestures with her arms. "Now *this* is my favorite room in the apartment."

Lila had to agree on this point, although there wasn't much competition. The bedroom was half the size of the other room, but painted white. It was empty except for a small desk in the corner and a braided rug on the floor.

"This space is completely versatile—during the day, you can use it for whatever you want."

"What if I want to sleep?" Bruce asked, rubbing his sore forehead. "Where's the bed?"

The agent smiled triumphantly. "Right here." She pulled on a rope that was connected to a wood panel in the wall. The panel gradually lowered, and a mattress appeared from behind it. "It's like having an extra room. You can put all kinds of things in here during the day, just as long as you move it all out into the other room before you go to sleep at night."

Lila's mouth hung open. Wall beds, kitchen bathtubs—it was more than she could take.

"We can't even see the beach from here," Bruce said, looking out the bedroom window. "That huge place across the street is blocking our view."

"I bet they have an incredible view." Lila pouted.

Mrs. Parker pushed the bed back into the wall. "You could sign the lease tomorrow and move in before the weekend, if you want to," she said. "Are you interested?"

Lila looked sadly at Bruce. As much as she wanted to move in with him, there was no way she could survive living in a place like this. It was too much to ask.

Bruce looked around, then looked back at Lila. "Actually, we are interested," he said confidently. "But not in this place. Show us the house across the street."

"Jess, did you hear me?" Elizabeth demanded. She finished putting away her fresh, neatly folded laundry, then went over to see what it was that captivated her sister's attention.

"Huh?" Jessica answered vaguely, not looking up from the book she was reading.

Elizabeth pounced on Jessica's bed. Jessica didn't move. Elizabeth started straightening the piles of books and papers that cluttered Jessica's desk. Normally Jessica found this incredibly annoying, but she didn't seem to notice. Elizabeth stopped what she was doing and stared at her. "Okay, what did you do with my sister?"

Jessica tore her eyes away from the book. "Liz, what on earth are you talking about?"

"You don't fool me—I know you're not the real Jessica Wakefield," she teased. "First you stay in on Friday night and then you sit there, completely involved in this enormous book. Obviously you've kidnapped Jessica and are attempting to impersonate her. I've got news for you—you're not doing a very good job."

Jessica rolled her eyes. "Har-har—very funny, Liz."

Elizabeth lifted the book to get a glimpse of the cover. "What book is so interesting that you can't put it down?"

Jessica sighed heavily, as if she'd been asked the same question a thousand times before. "For your information, I'm reading my Medieval History homework," she answered.

"Medieval history?" Elizabeth said, looking shocked and impressed at the same time. "I thought you wanted nothing to do with that class. You were absolutely determined to drop it."

Jessica carefully slipped a leather bookmark between the pages. "I changed my mind. It didn't seem so bad after all."

Elizabeth stood there, hands on hips, her mouth twitching as if she were about to burst into laughter.

Jessica frowned. *Why is it so hard to believe?* she wondered. Why couldn't anyone accept the fact that she had an intellectual side? It just took a while to come out. "I can change my mind, can't I?" she added defensively.

Elizabeth shrugged. "Sure, you can do whatever you want."

Jessica knew Elizabeth wasn't convinced, but she was grateful that her twin decided to drop it.

Elizabeth walked over to her desk and gathered

her books. "Before you become completely immersed in your work again, I just wanted to let you know that I'm going to the station to answer phones. Do I need to take my key?"

"I'll be here," Jessica mumbled, shaking her head.

Elizabeth stopped in the doorway. "Actually, I think I'll take it just in case," she said, reaching for her key ring. "You might change your mind again."

Jessica waved her sister out of the room. Finally she was alone. Jessica opened the book to where she had left off.

Eleanor of Aquitaine married Henry II of England in 1152. Jessica wondered what Eleanor's daily life was like. Jessica imagined herself dressed in thick velvet robes, with a jeweled crown on her head. Her days would be spent being waited on by servants and receiving guests. Knights would come from all over the world to ask for her hand in marriage, but she would refuse them. Her heart belonged to Henry, who Jessica imagined would look like Louis. She would wait patiently until he returned from battle, then she would run to the castle gates, royal blue robes and golden hair flying behind her. They would embrace, and he would say nothing, but his eyes would tell her how much he had missed her.

"Enough daydreaming," Jessica said out loud, bringing herself back to reality. She propped up her pillows and sat up. The problem with reading medieval history was that it always set her in a spiral of fantasies. It wasn't just happening during the day, either—many of Jessica's nights were spent by the castle gates, waiting for Louis.

Jessica leaned over her book, causing a golden strand of hair to fall across the pages. She smoothed back her hair, tucking the strand behind her ear. Suddenly she remembered her encounter with Louis at the water fountain. Jessica closed her eyes for a moment, recalling how he had gently touched her ear. It had been a very subtle gesture that would probably be meaningless to anyone else, but to Jessica it had felt like pure magic. Did he feel it too?

"Stop it!" Jessica scolded herself. For someone who had sworn off romance, she wasn't doing a very good job of it. She clicked on the radio and tuned in to a rock station to drown out her thoughts.

The music played, but still it wasn't enough to keep her mind from drifting. *I wonder if he's on campus today,* Jessica thought. She reached for the volume knob and turned the radio up another notch.

Is he in his office right now? What's he doing? The music still wasn't loud enough to get her mind off Louis. Jessica turned the radio up higher.

The speakers boomed, making the bookshelves vibrate. At first it seemed to be working, then thoughts of Louis slowly crept in. *Where did he come from?* she wondered. *Why did he come to Sweet Valley? Where does he live?*

There was a banging noise coming from the room next door. "Turn it down!" someone yelled.

Jessica clicked off the radio. "Sorry!" she shouted back. *I guess they're not into loud music,* Jessica thought wryly as she took a seat at her desk. *I wonder if Louis likes loud music.*

"Oh, no." Jessica sighed to herself, holding her head in her hands. Nothing could get Louis out of her mind, his face and gestures and voice were so imprinted on her brain. And that could only mean one thing. Jessica was falling for him.

Elizabeth slammed her book shut after reading the same page over again for the fifth time. The station was so quiet, Elizabeth swore she could hear the second hand of the clock as it swept around the dial.

She'd thought the solitude of the station would be the perfect place to get some studying done, but she couldn't concentrate. And yet strangely enough, Jessica was sitting in their room at that very moment, getting all of her work done. It was almost as if someone had broken into their room while they were asleep and secretly drained Elizabeth of her focus, then injected it all into her sister.

While she had no real explanation for why Jessica had suddenly been able to concentrate on her studies, Elizabeth at least understood why she herself couldn't. It was Tom. Ever since their fight, Elizabeth had hardly been able to think of anything else. After he'd left the station, he had gone back to his room to finish packing and then rushed off to catch his flight without stopping by to see her. He called her from a pay phone at the airport to say good-bye.

The memory of it made Elizabeth's eyes well up with tears. She was angry at him, but missed him at the same time. The hollow, empty feeling in her chest continued to grow. She wished he were there right now so the aching would go away. But the way things were going lately, she doubted that just his presence could fill the hole inside her. There were still some problems that they needed to work out.

Elizabeth dried her eyes and glanced at the dusty boxes of financial records in the corner. It made her so mad when she thought of how he left such a boring project for her to do, especially when she had better ideas to work with. It was a complete waste of time. Still, there was a nagging feeling in the back of her mind that maybe she'd overreacted just a bit. After all, he *had* been incredibly busy before he left. If she had been in his shoes, she might have done the very same thing.

Elizabeth walked over to the stack of boxes. She definitely had no intention of doing all the work, but maybe she could at least start the research. Then Tom could finish up when he returned. *If this relationship is going to work, I'll have to meet him halfway,* Elizabeth decided.

She examined the boxes. They were stained

and smelled of mildew, as if they had been stored in a damp basement for years. Elizabeth pushed up the sleeves of her SVU sweatshirt and moved them one by one, trying to find the box with the least amount of dirt. At the very bottom of the pile was a blue box that was a little larger than all the others and looked almost brand-new. It was marked ATHLETICS FINANCIAL FILES—CONFIDENTIAL in bold black letters. "I guess you're the one," Elizabeth said aloud, hoisting it onto a worktable.

She opened the box. Inside were files, stored haphazardly, their contents spilling out of the folders. Elizabeth quickly flipped through the pile, noticing that several pages of the ledger books were missing. Others were torn in half. Everything was in disarray. "How am I supposed to make sense out of this?" she cried in frustration.

Elizabeth dug her way to the bottom of the box, where she found a red folder marked DONATIONS. She opened the file and spread out the contents onto the worktable. Before her were several sheets of paper listing the names of five alumni who had donated $500,000 each over the last four years. *Am I missing something?* Elizabeth wondered as she reread the file. Didn't Tom say that the dean was on his case because SVU hadn't received a large alumni donation in several years?

Elizabeth added up the donations column. According to the records, the athletics department had received ten million dollars over the last four years. If that wasn't a large donation, what was?

Elizabeth switched on Tom's computer and connected to the university's database. She hoped the alumni computer files could give her some information about the donors and shed some light on the numbers she'd just discovered.

ARNOLD WALKER . . . Elizabeth typed into the computer. She waited a few moments for the system to search for his name. It popped up on the screen. Elizabeth typed FILE to get information. A moment later the computer beeped and the words INFORMATION NOT AVAILABLE flashed on the screen.

Elizabeth wrinkled her nose. "That's strange," she said to herself as she typed in the next name. That file was closed too. One by one, she discovered that none of the records could be accessed.

Elizabeth scanned the financial records again. She looked over the document closely and noticed an entry in the disbursement column that she didn't see before. In light pencil, written next to the donation amounts, was the word *discretionary*.

What does this mean? Elizabeth sat back in her chair and rubbed her forehead. Something wasn't quite right, but she couldn't pin it down. There could be any number of reasons why the alumni files weren't available, or that the financial files were a mess, or that a large donation was received without publicity. But it was the combination that didn't sit right with Elizabeth. Something was amiss. She could feel it in the pit of her stomach.

Suddenly the phone rang, startling Elizabeth. She hoped it was Tom so she could tell him how sorry she was about everything, and so she could share her discovery with him.

"Hello?" she said anxiously into the receiver.

"Is this WSVU?" a woman at the other end of the line asked.

"Yes . . ." Elizabeth tried to hide the disappointment in her voice. "May I help you?"

"This is Margaret McKee in Dr. Beal's office. We're in the process of moving into the new administrative offices, and we seemed to have misplaced some very important file boxes. We were wondering if any might have been sent to WSVU by mistake."

Elizabeth glanced at the open box in front of her. "What do they look like?"

"They're blue cardboard boxes marked athletics financial files. Do you have them?" Margaret asked.

"Let me take a quick look." Elizabeth held the receiver in her hand, wondering what to do. There was no doubt in her mind that the box on the table was one of the boxes they were looking for. She glanced down at the files. They didn't belong to her—she had no right to keep them. But what if this turned out to be something big? What if she was on the brink of uncovering a huge scandal? It would be wrong to let the perpetrators go unpunished. Besides, the last thing she wanted to do was to have an important story slip through her fingers.

"I'm sorry," Elizabeth said firmly as she closed the cardboard box. "We don't have your files."

Chapter
Eight

"Elizabeth?" Todd said with surprise as he opened the door. "Come on in. It's good to see you."

Elizabeth walked into Todd's dorm room. It was almost like stepping back in time, to when they had first arrived on campus and were still a couple. Not much had changed since then, except for the Lakers poster being taken off the wall and Todd's basketball trophies missing from the bookshelf.

"Have a seat," Todd said, motioning to the small sofa by the window. He was dressed in shorts and an old T-shirt, and his hair was a mess. The blinds were drawn, and even though it was a bright, sunny day, the light in the room was hazy and gray. Elizabeth sat down while Todd took a seat at his desk. "So what brings you here?" he asked.

"Gin-Yung told me what happened. I'm sorry they won't let you back on the team," she said sympathetically.

"Thanks for saying that." Todd looked down at the floor. "It means a lot."

Elizabeth's throat tightened as she watched him. He seemed so sad. "In a way, I feel partially responsible. . . ."

Todd shook his head. "Don't feel that way, Elizabeth. It's not your fault."

Elizabeth looked back at the empty bookshelf. "I can't help it. If I hadn't opened the investigation on preferential treatment, this never would have happened to you," she said guiltily.

"We've been through this before. You were doing your job—you did what you thought was right. *I'm* the one at fault. I never should've accepted the preferential treatment to begin with." Todd squeezed his hand into a solid fist. "But I've paid my dues. I made it up to everyone—there's no reason why I shouldn't be allowed back on the team for next season."

Elizabeth noticed that Todd's face looked weary. There were dark circles under his eyes, and his complexion was pale. She had never seen him so distraught before. "Is there anyone else you can talk to? Someone with influence who could help you?"

"No—I don't think so. The head of the athletics department, Coach Crane, is the one who turned down my request, so he's definitely out." Todd ran his fingers through his tousled hair. "I doubt there's really anything Coach Shultz back at Sweet Valley High can do."

She walked over to the window and opened the

blinds partway, allowing a few yellow beams of sunlight to pour in. *There has to be someone else who can help Todd.* Elizabeth thought hard. Other than faculty, who would have influence on the school? Then she remembered the cardboard box of financial files she had seen the night before at the station. "What about donors?"

"Donors?" Todd asked in bewilderment. "I don't follow you."

Elizabeth sat back down on the couch. "Maybe you could talk to someone who's donated a lot of money to the athletics department. If you can get the donors on your side, maybe the athletics department would reconsider. People with money can be very influential."

Todd scratched his head. "That's a good idea, except for one thing. There aren't any donors."

Elizabeth's heart skipped a beat. "What do you mean?"

"The athletics department doesn't have any money. They're nearly broke. The floor of the basketball court is in bad shape and the lockers are almost all broken. Coach Crane is always complaining that there isn't enough funding," he said.

Elizabeth's eyes narrowed. Pictures of the financial ledger flashed through her mind. "Are you sure there aren't any alumni who donate money to the department?"

Todd lifted his head and looked directly into her eyes. "Positive."

*   *   *

"Come on, Winnie—we'll go to the early show," Denise pleaded between sips of cappuccino. "We'll be back before nine."

Winston looked around the bustling coffee-house. A waitress dressed completely in black zig-zagged through the maze of wooden tables, her silver earrings swinging as she walked. She was carrying a tray filled with tiny white cups. Winston caught her eye and motioned for her to come over. "I *can't*, Denise. I'd love to, but I can't."

The waitress stopped in front of him, gracefully balancing the edge of the tray with her shoulder. Winston noticed that even her short fingernails were painted black. "What can I get you?" she asked.

"A double espresso—and a bacon cheeseburger," Winston answered without opening the menu.

"Gotcha." The waitress hurried off to another table.

Denise smiled at Winston. "The movie's only two hours long—you can study afterward."

Winston sighed as he looked at her. How could someone so beautiful cause him so much grief? "You know what'll happen. After the movie, you'll have a craving for a hot-fudge sundae or something. We'll get to the ice-cream place and we'll bump into some friends of yours. And the next thing you know, we'll be dancing up a storm at an all-night party."

"Sounds fun!" Denise's laughter made Winston think of champagne being poured into fine crystal. "But seriously, Winnie—I promise it won't happen this time."

Winston stared into her soft, pleading eyes. His body went limp. Already he could feel his resolve breaking down. "Don't do this to me, Denise. I'm so far behind right now, I'd be lucky to get a C on the exam."

Denise rested her hand on his. "You're being too hard on yourself, Win. Your eyes are blood-shot, you're slumped in your chair—you look exhausted. Are you taking good care of yourself?"

"Of course I am," Winston answered tiredly.

The waitress reappeared, carrying a plate and a tiny cup. "Bacon cheeseburger and double espresso—" She set them in front of Winston. The moment she turned away, Winston dove into his food.

"This is what I'm talking about," Denise said, pointing to his lunch. "A double shot of caffeine and a quarter pound of grease isn't what I call taking care of yourself."

"I haven't been getting much sleep lately," Winston said through a mouthful of food. "I need an energy rush. I'm just doing what I can to survive."

Denise finished her cappuccino. "I think you're too stressed about this whole thing. You need to relax a little more. Have you been doing those breathing exercises I taught you?"

He shook his head. "It's not that simple." Winston wiped his mouth with a napkin. "I don't think you realize what's at stake here, Denise. My parents have always been really strict about grades

111

and education. Just before I came to SVU, my dad told me that college wasn't for fun—it was for getting a degree. He said that if my grades got bad, he'd stop paying for school."

"What are you trying to tell me?"

"If my dad doesn't pay, I'm going to have to transfer to a community college, which means it won't be so easy to see each other anymore."

Denise chewed her lower lip. "That's not cool. What should we do?"

Winston took a sip of the strong coffee. "I think there's only one thing we *can* do," he said seriously. "Let's try to stay away from each other—at least until the exam is over. Please do this for me."

"Okay, whatever you need to do, Winnie," Denise answered solemnly. "I'll support you."

Winston pulled off the top of his burger and removed the pickles. "Thanks. Just make sure you do it from a distance." He smiled with relief. He was glad that she understood. Now he would be able to study without any distractions.

Denise popped the pickle slices in her mouth. "I guess I'll ask Anoushka if she wants to go to the movies tonight," she said. She leaned over and planted a kiss on Winston's cheek. "But it won't be the same."

"Go and have a great time." Just as the words escaped him, he was overcome with a feeling of loss. It wasn't that he didn't want her to have fun, but he wished he could be there to share it with her. Studying for the physics exam was going to be tough. But not nearly as tough as being separated from the woman he loved.

The sun shone brightly on the quad, and there wasn't a cloud in sight. It was the perfect day to be outside. Everyone was out, except for the few unfortunate souls who were stuck in classes. Volleyball nets and Frisbees were brought outside, blankets were spread out on the grass. Study groups formed in tight little circles on the lawn, taking advantage of every bit of warm sunlight.

Jessica decided early on that she wasn't going to spend the day inside. Even though she had intended to get some serious studying in, there was nothing she had to do that couldn't be done outdoors. She searched the quad for a secluded spot, where she wouldn't be in the middle of a Frisbee game or get hit by a volleyball. She settled near a tree, in a quiet corner of the quad.

Jessica comfortably stretched out on the green grass. *This is the ideal place to sit and read medieval history,* she thought happily. She slipped her feet out of her sandals and rolled up the cuffs of her shorts. If she was going to spend a sunny afternoon reading a book, she might as well work on her tan, too.

Jessica laid her notebook beside her and cracked open the history book. The assignment for the next class was to read to the end of the third chapter, but Jessica had become so engrossed in the

113

reading that she had read through most of the fourth. That section was about chivalry—the code of conduct for knights. Jessica was absolutely amazed by the way they courted women in the Middle Ages. It wasn't out of the ordinary for them to carry a woman over a puddle so her feet wouldn't get wet or to fight to the death with a rival for a woman's hand. True knights were absolutely obsessed with the women they loved. Jessica had even read the story of a man who had traveled for many miles on a cart piled with dead bodies because it was the fastest way to get to his true love.

Jessica sighed. Where did all the knights go? No one risked themselves for love anymore. She was convinced that when chivalry died out, romance went along with it. Jessica wished she'd been born in the Middle Ages, when real romance was alive and well. She was certain she would've been able to find her true love.

Jessica's reverie was broken by a strong gust of wind that blew across the quad. Her notebook fluttered open, and the pages inside scattered over the lawn. Jessica scrambled to pick up the papers. Another gust came up, tossing the pages like tumbleweed.

Jessica chased the papers, collecting as many as she could. When she picked up the last one, she realized the stack was thin. It was only a third of the papers she'd originally had in her notebook. She looked around, but the notes were nowhere to be found. All the work she'd done over the past few days was gone.

"Great. Just great." Jessica plopped down at the base of the tree, trying to sort the pile.

"Are you looking for these?"

She turned and saw Louis standing next to her, holding the rest of her notes in his hand. Jessica stared at him in shock. She had been thinking about him so much the past few days that seeing him for real caught her off guard. "Thanks," she answered breathlessly as she tucked the papers into her notebook.

"See? Chivalry isn't dead after all," he said as he put down his briefcase.

Jessica's heart began to pound. Why did he have to be so handsome? "Chivalry may not be dead, but it's definitely on sick leave," she said ruefully. "I think all the knights have gone into hiding."

Louis smiled brightly, straightening his tie knot. "There are still a few of us around," he joked.

Jessica laughed. It was comforting to be here, talking to him like this. "The men I've dated could certainly take a few lessons," she said harshly, surprised by the sound of her own voice.

Louis's forehead wrinkled. "If you don't mind me saying so, you seem too young to be so bitter."

Jessica leaned back against the trunk of the tree and looked into the distance. She felt herself opening up, ready to tell him anything he wanted to know about her life. "I've been hurt too many times. Whenever I thought I'd found true love, it turned out that there was nothing real about it. It's not worth the heartache. I've given up on love altogether."

"Don't do that," Louis said with an urgency that caught her off guard. His lips formed a tight line. "The worst thing you can do is lose hope. When life brings us to the edge of despair, hope is the one thing we can hold on to."

Their eyes locked. His green eyes stared at her with an astonishing intensity, but Jessica couldn't seem to break away. She felt as if they were drawing her down further into their swirling depths.

"Look at the legend of Tristan and Iseult, for example," he began, his eyes still fixed on her. His voice was deep and steady. "Tristan and Iseult were lovers who were forced to live separated from each other. One day Tristan was critically wounded in battle. He knew that the sight of his beloved Iseult would heal him, so he sent a ship for her."

Jessica listened closely, trying to absorb every detail—the exact words he used, the sound of his voice, the way he looked at her. She wanted to hold on to every second, because she knew she wouldn't be able to think of anything else until the next time she saw him.

Louis continued. "He told the sailors to fly a white mast on their ship if Iseult had agreed to return with them, so that he would know the answer immediately when he saw the ship on the horizon. If she wasn't on the ship, they were ordered to fly a black sail. Then he waited."

"What happened next?" Jessica whispered, barely able to breathe. "Did she go to him?"

"What happened isn't as important as the fact that Tristan never gave up on his true love. Even though he was dying, he waited in hope."

Jessica shook her head. "Okay, okay—I get the point about hope. But what happened? Was Iseult on the ship?" she asked desperately.

Louis's face suddenly brightened, and his eyes sparkled with delight. "Caught your interest, did I? Tell you what, I'm going to give the class an assignment to research a legend and write an essay about it. Why don't you do yours on Tristan and Iseult?"

Jessica groaned. She felt like someone had just placed an exquisite jewel in the palm of her hand, then suddenly ripped it away. "You're going to make me research the rest of the story? Why don't you just tell me the end now, and then I'll write about it?" she answered slyly.

Louis picked up his briefcase. "Nice try, Jessica. I'm sure you'll have no trouble finding the story in any book on Arthurian legends," he said as he started walking up the path. "I'll see you in class."

"Bye," she said reluctantly. She tried to quickly think of something to say to keep the conversation going, anything to make him stop and turn around again, but the words escaped her.

Jessica watched his tall frame walk across the quad, and she was filled with longing. *Does he feel it too?* she wondered. There was that one moment, when he stared deeply into her eyes, that Jessica was certain he shared the same feelings. It was too strong to be one-sided. Or was she imagining things?

Jessica's head was spinning. She wanted to believe that he was attracted to her, but what if she was wrong? She had to know. Her heart wouldn't survive another break.

That was a close one. Louis breathed a sigh of relief as he headed across the quad. For a moment, it seemed as though his conversation with Jessica was about to get too personal. It'd come upon him so suddenly, he'd hardly been aware of it. It had seemed so natural to talk openly with her. Fortunately he realized what was happening before things got out of hand. With a little maneuvering, he had managed to steer the conversation in the proper direction.

Still, he couldn't stop wondering what had made her so jaded when it came to love. Who had treated her so badly? He imagined the boys that had floated in and out of Jessica's life, too selfish to give of themselves. It made him angry to think of the immature kids stomping on Jessica's heart, without giving it a second thought. She didn't deserve to be treated that way, and somehow he found himself wanting to protect her from it.

Louis ducked to avoid a Frisbee that was coming straight for his head.

"Sorry about that!" a young man in plaid

shorts and a baseball cap said as he caught the Frisbee.

"It's all right," Louis answered. He fought back the urge to throw off his tie, roll up his sleeves, and join the game. He didn't want to leave the campus. There was so much life and chatter going on all around him. It was a stark contrast to the lonely house that awaited him. If only he could stick around and play Frisbee in the sunshine or sit and talk with Jessica for the rest of the afternoon.

You're a professor, not a student, in case you've forgotten, he scolded himself harshly. He had come to Sweet Valley to start a new life and to build his career. It was important to stay focused on his job and to be a good teacher. Part of being a good teacher was developing friendly relationships with his students. But there was a danger in becoming too close. Louis already felt the stirrings of an attraction toward Jessica. He'd have to work hard to keep his feelings under control or his career would be in jeopardy.

Louis continued on past the Frisbee game, on his way to the parking lot. As long as he kept himself busy with work, going home would be bearable. He certainly had enough work to keep him from feeling the loneliness. There was a lecture to plan and chapters he had to read in order to prepare for his next class. It was enough to get him through the night.

Suddenly Louis stopped in his tracks. His briefcase

felt unusually light. *Did I bring the book with me?* He suddenly remembered that he had left it on the desk in his office. He'd have to go back and get it. He sighed wearily and turned around.

As he looked down the path, he caught a glimpse of Jessica staring at him. He looked back at her, and their eyes met. Louis started to tremble. He walked toward her, slowly, as if being drawn by some strange magnetic force. Jessica seemed startled and looked away, bending her head over her book. Louis faced straight ahead and hurried past her, on his way back to the office.

Chapter Nine

"Coach Crane, could I speak with you for a moment?" Elizabeth asked as she stood in the doorway of the athletics office. Her knees started to shake. Whenever Elizabeth was nervous, she tried to imagine how her favorite journalist, Angela Hunter, would handle the situation.

"What do you want?" the aging coach said in a gruff tone.

Elizabeth cleared her throat. She pulled back her shoulders and spoke in her most professional, journalistic voice. "I'm sorry to bother you. I'm working on a piece for WSVU, and I'd like to ask you a few questions."

The coach lifted his baseball cap and scratched the top of his bald head. "Sure. Publicity for the athletics program is always a good thing," he said abruptly. "Have a seat, Ms.—"

"Wakefield," Elizabeth finished. She took a

seat and smoothed the pleats of her navy blue skirt. Getting an interview with Crane was a lot easier than she'd expected. After blowing the cover off the preferential treatment scandal, she'd thought he would never let her back into his office again.

"You look familiar to me," the coach said, wagging a thick finger at her. "Do you play on any of the sports teams?"

"No, I don't," Elizabeth answered quickly. He didn't remember her, and that was a good sign. But Elizabeth was sure it wouldn't take too long for him to put the pieces together. She didn't have much time. "I know you're a busy man, so I don't want to keep you. I just have a few questions to ask."

Coach Crane laced his fingers behind his head and leaned back in his chair. "Fire away."

Elizabeth gazed down at her notebook. It was blank, but she needed something to look at besides Crane's cold stare. "The story I'm working on is about the importance of alumni donations. I understand the athletics department hasn't received a major donation in quite some time. When was the last significant donation you received?"

The coach's eyes were distant. He seemed lost in thought. Elizabeth glanced nervously at the game schedule posted on the wall. She hoped the memory of their last interview wasn't coming back to him. "Coach?" Elizabeth spoke gingerly. "Did you hear my question?"

"Yes—yes, of course," he said. There was a

troubled look in his eyes. "I don't really recall."

"I just need a ballpark estimate. Was it within the last five years? Ten years, maybe?" Elizabeth persisted.

The coach leaned forward, elbows on his desk. His plump belly was stretching his striped jersey to its maximum limit. "The years fly by so fast, I can hardly keep track of things," he said with an anxious laugh. "I just don't remember."

"That's all right; dates are hard to remember," she said lightly as she doodled in her notebook. "What was the amount of the last contribution?"

The coach puckered his lips thoughtfully. Deep furrows appeared over his brow. "That's hard to say. It was so long ago—"

Elizabeth eyed him skeptically. Angela Hunter would've definitely taken that answer as a warning flag. Money was always the driving force in university programs, especially athletics. How could he forget a major contribution? "There must be some financial records that could give us a few clues," she suggested, a bit more forcefully this time. "You do keep records of your donations, don't you?"

He glared at her. "Of course we do, Ms. Wakefield," the coach said with patronizing smile. "There are plenty of records, but right now we are in the middle of renovations, like the rest of this campus. It would be impossible to locate the information right now."

This is going nowhere. What was he trying to hide? She stood up. "Maybe I should come back later when things are more organized."

Coach Crane stood too and showed her to the door. He seemed relieved. The creases in his forehead disappeared, and his mouth showed a hint of kindness. "Certainly. We'd be more than happy to give you the information you need. Good luck on your story."

"Thanks," Elizabeth said stiffly as she walked out the door. *That was strange,* she thought as she turned down the hall. At first he seemed so eager for department publicity, and then he wouldn't give her any information. If he didn't know anything, there had to be someone around here who did. Elizabeth made a note on her pad: *Make arrangements to speak with someone in accounting office.*

Elizabeth was too busy writing in her notebook to see the cardboard boxes that were stacked in the middle of the hallway. She looked up from her notebook a second too late—just as she slammed her knee into one of the boxes.

"OW!" she yelled, dropping her notebook and grabbing her throbbing knee. Whose bright idea was it to leave boxes in the middle of a hallway? Pain shot through her knee as she felt a bruise swelling.

As she bent down unsteadily to retrieve her notebook, she noticed the box she'd run into. It was a blue cardboard box, similar to the one she'd been looking through at the station. The word FI-NANCIAL was printed in bold black letters. Elizabeth peered into the box, which held piles of computer disks. Her gut told her there was a good chance that the information she was looking for was on one of those disks. She looked over her shoulder to see if anyone was coming, then reached in and took a stack of disks from the box.

Maybe this trip hasn't been a complete waste of time after all, Elizabeth thought as she threw them into her bag. She thanked her aching knee for making the discovery and hobbled triumphantly toward the elevator.

"It's lunchtime!" Winston shouted with victory as he slammed shut his book. He had one hour to relax, and then he'd have to hit the books again. He figured that if he allowed himself a few breaks in between studying, he'd get more work done. So far, his system was working—he'd actually finished an entire problem set without help from anyone in his study group.

Winston searched through a pile of dirty laundry until he located his telephone. He was going to call Denise. Since he was officially on break, there was no reason why they couldn't get together for a little while. He dialed the number as quickly as his fingers could move. It had been exactly twenty-four hours since the last time he'd seen her, but it felt like forever.

The phone rang three times, but there was no answer. "Come on, Denise, I know you're there . . . pick up the phone," Winston said into the receiver. He pushed a stack of papers and books onto the floor, leaned back in his chair, and rested his feet on the desktop. The phone kept on ringing.

Finally there was a click. "Hi, this is Denise . . . leave me a message and I'll get back to you soon. If this is Winnie, hang up the phone and get back to work!" Then there was a beep.

"Denise, this is Winston . . . I just wanted to know if you wanted to get together for lunch . . . I called a couple of times last night, but you didn't get back to me . . . I'm heading over to the dining hall in about three minutes. Call me if you want to go." Winston paused for a moment. "Miss you. Bye."

He hung up the phone. He wondered if she'd been in her room, listening to him leaving the message. Winston wrung his hands nervously. *Why hasn't she called me back?* He hoped she wasn't mad at him about needing to spend some time apart. It wasn't like he wanted to do it. It was just that he didn't have any other choice.

Winston put on his jacket, then sat by the phone, waiting patiently for it to ring. *Please call.* All he needed was to see Denise for a few minutes, and then he'd be fine. He just wanted to know that she wasn't mad at him, then he'd be able to study for the rest of the afternoon. If she didn't call, he wouldn't be able to concentrate on his work. Instead he'd spend the entire afternoon wondering why she never got back to him. Then he wouldn't get anything done. The whole situation made him crazy.

Winston waited for ten minutes before his

growling stomach made him give up. *She's not going to call,* he realized sadly as he left for the dining hall. There was empty feeling inside him that was mixed with intense frustration. It was like a chunk of him was missing, and even though he knew exactly where it was, he couldn't get it back.

"It's a gorgeous day out!" Nina proclaimed as she poked her head into the station office. "So why are you spending it in front of a boring old computer screen?"

Elizabeth shuffled through the pile of the computer disks she'd swiped from the athletics department. It was turning out to be a bit more work than she'd expected. Out of the entire stack of disks, only a few of them were labeled. "I have a lot of work to catch up on now that Tom's away," she answered.

Nina stepped inside the office. She was wearing cutoffs and a gold tank top that looked great against her brown skin. She lifted her sunglasses and stuck them on top of her head. "Remember how you told me that Tom was working too hard? It looks like you're doing the exact same thing. I guess you two really are made for each other." Nina's braids clicked as she shook her head. "Why don't you take a break? We can grab a couple of salads and have lunch on the quad. If you don't mind me saying so, I think you could use a little sunshine."

Elizabeth looked down at her pale arms. Her

tan was fading. Between studying and working at the station, she hadn't had a chance to spend much time outside. "I'd love to, but I can't right now. I have to check up on some things and then I have to pick up Jessica's shirt from the dry cleaner's. Maybe we can do it tomorrow." Elizabeth popped one of the disks into the computer.

"Whenever you're ready," Nina said casually. She leaned over Elizabeth's shoulder and looked at the screen. "Are you on the trail of some hot story?"

Elizabeth searched through the computer files listed on the menu. "Actually, I am onto something interesting, but I can't fill you in on the details until I know more about what's going on. I *can* tell you that it involves that crummy assignment Tom left me. It seems to be more involved than either of us thought."

Nina whistled. "I can't wait to hear about this one." She turned on her heels and headed for the door. "Take it easy, Lois Lane. Give me a call when you feel like lunch."

"I will. Catch a few rays for me."

Nina winked at her. "You bet."

Elizabeth heard the door close. She ejected the disk. It didn't have any of the information she was looking for. As the pile of unchecked disks diminished, the pile of useless disks continued to grow.

Elizabeth popped in the last disk. She scanned the menu, and her eyes rested on a file marked DONORS. *I hope this is the one I need,* she thought.

Elizabeth opened the file. Instantly the names of the five donors appeared on the screen. "Bingo!" she shouted.

Her body tensed in anticipation. A spreadsheet covered the screen, with payments listed, just like they had been on the ledger. But this time there was an extra column. She leaned closer and peered at the screen. From what she could gather, it explained where the money from each donation had been spent.

Elizabeth read the list aloud. "Reflooring of the basketball court, new gym lockers, renovations to the athletics department offices . . ." Next to the column were the dates that all the projects had been completed. Elizabeth shrank back. It all seemed normal and routine. There was nothing out of the ordinary here.

Suddenly it hit her like a bolt of lightning on a clear day. "Wait a minute . . ." She took a closer look at the dates. She reached down and touched the bruise on her knee that she'd gotten by running into that stack of boxes outside Crane's office. The pieces weren't fitting together. "If they're doing renovations to the athletics building right now, how could they have been completed a year ago?"

Elizabeth flashed back to her conversation with Todd. Didn't he say the basketball floor was in bad need of repair? Didn't he say the lockers needed to be replaced? According to the computer records, both were replaced six months ago.

Something strange is definitely going on here, Elizabeth decided. She scratched her head thoughtfully. Things just didn't add up. The department was practically broke, but it had supposedly received substantial donations every year for the past four years. Coach Crane couldn't recall any information about it, and Todd said that he'd never heard of any donors. How could they not know anything about it? Crane was in over his head after the preferential treatment scandal, and Elizabeth could understand why he wouldn't tell her the truth. But Todd was another story. What was he trying to hide?

"If Professor Miles isn't here in five minutes, I'm leaving!" shouted one of the students in Jessica's Medieval History class.

"Why wait that long?" someone else answered from across the room. "He's already fifteen minutes late."

A few people nodded. It was an unwritten rule at SVU that if the professor was more than fifteen minutes late, the students didn't have to stay. The amount of time actually varied from class to class. Film seminar students would wait almost a full twenty minutes before they thought about leaving. But the Medieval History crowd was completely different. They'd begun trickling out after waiting only ten minutes.

A woman who sat across the aisle from Jessica got up to leave. *It's only been thirteen and a half minutes,* Jessica told herself silently. Jessica stayed glued to her seat. She wasn't about to move until she was absolutely sure Louis wasn't coming.

Another minute passed. A cluster of people left, happy at the unexpected surprise of having no class. But Jessica felt differently. The heaviness of disappointment started to creep up on her. She had been looking forward to this class in particular and to seeing him again. She'd spent last night in the library, doing research for her essay and finishing it so she could hand it in for today's class. Jessica wanted to impress Louis by turning it in early. Now he'd never know how hard she'd worked. *Where are you, Louis?*

"I'm not waiting all day," a short girl in sweatpants said out loud. "I'm going to the gym." She pushed past Jessica and walked out of the room.

The last of the students walked out, and soon Jessica was the only one left. *He's going to be here. I just know he is,* she tried to convince herself. Jessica's silver bracelets tinkled as she smoothed the wrinkles in her blue-green sheath dress. It was her favorite. She had worn it because it brought out the color of her eyes and looked pretty against her golden hair. She had hoped Louis would like it.

Jessica patiently watched the clock on the wall as the second hand circled around. Doubts seeped into her like poison. *What are you waiting for? He's not going to show. Why are you wasting your time? He's just a professor.* Jessica shook her head, trying to make the thoughts go away. He wasn't just a professor. Louis was the most fascinating man she had ever met. She knew that at any moment he would walk right through that door. She could feel it.

"I guess I didn't make it in time."

Jessica turned toward the doorway.

Louis was leaning against the wall, surveying the empty classroom. He was out of breath. "I had a little car trouble," he said, smiling at her. His tie was crooked and his hair was a mess, but he was still gorgeous. "It's nice to see that at least someone waited for me."

Jessica blinked to make sure she wasn't daydreaming. He was still standing there. "They couldn't wait," Jessica said as she brushed a strand of hair behind her ear. "But I didn't want to miss a single moment of Medieval History," she teased. Suddenly she wondered if it was a mistake to wait for him. Maybe staying made her feelings too obvious.

Louis set his briefcase down on the desk. "I guess there's no point in starting the lecture now. I'll have to save it for the next class." He opened the case and took out a book. His gentle hands touched it reverently, as if it were a sacred text. "While we're here, is there anything you want to go over? Is there anything you don't understand?"

Jessica approached the desk delicately, careful not to trip in her high heels. She felt herself unraveling, as though all the tension she had felt since their last meeting was coming undone. "I wanted to give you my essay on Tristan and Iseult."

"You're done already?" he said with surprise. His eyes were on her, cool and soothing. "That's quite impressive. Since we have some time to kill, why don't you read it aloud?" He gestured for Jessica to sit in his chair, while he sat casually on the edge of his desk.

Jessica took a deep breath and began to read. She could hear the sound of her heart thumping loudly in her chest and wondered in embarrassment if he could hear it too. Out of the corner of her eye she saw Louis gazing at her intently, listening to every word she said. She had his complete and undivided attention.

"Tristan waited day after day, knowing that soon he would see the white mast of the ship, and his lover, Iseult, would return to him.

"But weeks passed, and there was no sign of the ship. Tristan's strength faltered. Then one day, the white-masted ship was spotted by Iseult's rival, who was deeply in love with Tristan. At the first sight of the ship, she rushed to Tristan's bedside and told him that she'd spotted the ship. When he asked her the color of the mast, she lied, saying that it was black. Tristan was overcome with sorrow and died of a broken heart."

Jessica continued to read, feeling Louis moving toward her. Her heart pounded, sending hot blood to her cheeks. She swore she could feel the faint whisper of Louis's breath against her skin.

"Iseult arrived to find her lover dead. In her grief, she stretched out beside him and died. They were buried in adjoining graves, and from the ground grew a white briar and a red briar. The two entwined together as a symbol that their love was stronger than death."

When she finished, Jessica looked up at Louis, who was leaning over her. He was only inches away, and she could smell the sweet, earthy scent of his aftershave. "Very well done. It's a beautiful story. . . ." he said hoarsely.

Jessica nodded slowly. An invisible thread seemed to draw her closer and closer to him. She closed her eyes, the pounding of her heart resonating in her ears. She waited for the soft touch of his lips against hers.

There was a knock on the door. Jessica opened her eyes. A student was standing in the doorway. "Professor Miles? Can I talk to you for a minute?" he said.

Louis sat up, and Jessica watched as he expertly gathered his composure in a matter of seconds. "Certainly," he said in a scholarly tone. He turned to her. The softness she had seen in his eyes only seconds before took on a harder edge. "Jessica, why don't you leave your essay with me. I'll see you at the next class."

Jessica felt the color drain from her face. The pounding in her chest subsided. "Sure," she answered in confusion. She dropped the paper into his briefcase and slipped out the door.

The moment had come and gone so quickly, Jessica wondered if she had imagined it all. She wanted to stay, to wait for him again, to recapture the spark between them that had been stamped out too soon. Instead she walked out of the building, one foot in front of the other. Jessica's body moved on, but her heart lingered by the door, waiting for him. Her steps quickened. Everything about him was calling her to stay—the rough texture of his tweed coat, the curve of his shoulders, the way he smelled. They were all like ropes pulling against her, threatening to tear her in two.

Chapter
Ten

"Todd—open up!" Elizabeth shouted, knocking furiously on his door. Her knuckles started to hurt. *How can he do this to me?* All this time she'd felt sorry for him. She was willing to try and help him get back on the team, but he wasn't being straight with her. If Todd was hiding something, Elizabeth was determined to get to the bottom of it. "Open up!" she shouted.

The door opened, and Gin-Yung appeared in the doorway. She looked at her strangely. "Elizabeth—what's wrong?"

The wave of anger consuming Elizabeth dissolved at the sight of Gin-Yung. "Is Todd here?" she asked, lowering her voice.

Todd stood behind Gin-Yung. "I'm here, Liz." He squinted at her as if he were staring into the sun. "What's going on?"

Elizabeth glared at him, her eyes tinged

with fire. "Todd, we have to talk—*alone.*"

Todd's arm encircled Gin-Yung's waist protectively. "Is that all right with you?" he asked.

"That's fine," Gin-Yung said, still looking at Elizabeth. "I have to get to class anyway." She gave Todd a quick kiss and hurried out the door. "Call me later."

Elizabeth strolled in, and Todd closed the door forcefully behind them. "Okay, Liz. What's this all about? What's so urgent that you have to practically bang down my door in the middle of the afternoon?"

Elizabeth paced the room. She felt the blood coursing through her veins. "How do you expect me to help clear your name when you won't tell me the whole truth?"

"Liz, what are you talking about?" Todd looked directly into her eyes. "When did I lie to you?"

Elizabeth looked back at him, feeling as though she were staring at a stranger. They had shared so much together. She thought she knew him so well. But now she was beginning to wonder if she knew Todd at all. "You said there weren't any donors," she answered with exasperation. "Don't pretend you don't know what I'm talking about."

Todd sat down, slinging one leg casually over the arm of the chair. "What donors? You're not making any sense."

Elizabeth dropped the computer printout on his lap. "Come on, Todd. I'm talking about the

137

ten million dollars that the athletics department has received over the last four years. You were one of the top players. You must've known about it."

Todd picked up the pages, scanning the rows of numbers. "Ten million dollars? What is this?"

"Don't you recognize the names?" Elizabeth said, pointing to the list.

Todd shook his head. "I don't know who these people are, or what you think I'm supposedly hiding from you," he said earnestly. "Would you please tell me what is going on? And start from the beginning."

Elizabeth suddenly realized that the person she was speaking to was the same Todd she had always known. All it took was a simple glimmer in his eye or the turn of his head for her to know when he was telling the truth. He honestly had no idea about any of it. "I'm sorry," Elizabeth said softly. "I didn't mean to attack you like that. I guess I jumped to conclusions." She explained the whole story to him, including the mysterious files and her meeting with Coach Crane.

Todd listened carefully as she spoke. "I think you're right, Liz. Something fishy *is* going on," he said. "But don't you think I would have told you if I knew anything?"

Elizabeth nodded in embarrassment. "You're right. I'm sorry."

Todd gave her a bright smile. "You're forgiven." He looked over the computer printout and rubbed his chin thoughtfully. "I still can't believe these numbers. How could they keep this a secret? And why would they want to in the first place?"

"That's what I'm trying to figure out."

Todd leaned over and opened his mini-refrigerator. "Do you want something to drink? All I've got is soda."

"I'll take a cola." Elizabeth smiled as she took the can from him. She noticed that the window shades were pulled up, flooding the room in sunlight. She was glad to see that Todd was feeling better than the last time she'd seen him.

Todd popped open a can and took a drink. "We know from the records that the department received ten million dollars, but the money obviously hasn't been spent on equipment."

"Where could it have gone? Do you have any ideas?" Elizabeth asked.

Todd shook his head as he stared at the files. "I just keep thinking that it must've gone to line somebody's pockets."

Elizabeth nearly choked on her soda. There was a tingling at the base of her spine, a sense she always had when she was about to uncover something big. "Wait a minute—are you saying that someone has taken the money?"

"I'm saying it's a possibility," Todd answered seriously. "Or maybe the money was *given* to someone. If they were willing to do special favors for athletes like me, I wouldn't be surprised if they were willing to pay for them, too."

Elizabeth clutched the soda can in her hand as she absorbed the implications of what Todd was saying. If he was right, this could be the biggest break of her career.

Mrs. Parker spread her arms out wide, as if she were trying to hug the entire beach house. It had taken a couple of days, but she'd finally managed to round up the keys to the luxurious dwelling. "So what do you think so far?" she asked.

Lila and Bruce stood in the living room and gazed at everything before them. Lila slipped off her shoes and sank her toes deep into the plush white carpet. "It's an absolute dream," she said breathlessly.

Mrs. Parker touched the lizard pin that was perched on the lapel of her mint green business suit. "It *is* a splendid house—but it's a bit pricey. I think the other one might be more in line with your budget."

Lila walked past the enormous fireplace that stretched all the way to the cathedral ceiling. "Oh, look at all this space, Bruce. I just love the airy openness of it." There was no wall dividing the dining room and the living room, so that the main floor was completely free of barriers. From where she was standing, Lila could see the kitchen, with its glass and oak cabinets. It was fully equipped with a dishwasher and trash compactor. The stove even had a grill. An island with a wide countertop was in the center of the room. With stools lined up on one side, the island also doubled as a breakfast bar.

But what Lila loved the most were the windows. "And would you look at this view. This is absolute heaven."

The entire main floor was surrounded with glass, and no matter where you were, there was a breathtaking view of the beach. Light poured in from all directions, and the warmth felt good on Lila's skin.

Mrs. Parker started to climb the spiral staircase. "One thing to keep in mind is that this place does not come fully furnished. You might find that the other place is more suitable in that respect."

Lila ignored the comment, not allowing thoughts of that filthy dump to ruin her happiness. When they reached the top of the stairs, she glanced back at Bruce, who was looking over the wooden banister down at the main floor. Lila took a peek and felt woozy from the height. Bruce silently held her hand, and they followed Mrs. Parker down the hallway.

There were two guest rooms, a den, a laundry room—but Lila was completely taken with the master bedroom. She squeezed Bruce's hand tighter as they looked at it. "This is amazing. I bet this room is bigger than the entire apartment across the street," Lila said as she walked toward the master bathroom on one side of the room. It had dark green ceramic tile and brass fixtures, with a whirlpool bath. On the other side of the room Lila

141

found a walk-in closet that was almost the same size as her dorm room. Everything was perfect.

"Honey, come here," Bruce called in a soft voice. He'd pushed back the glass doors and stood on the balcony. Down below was the deck, which had a free-form swimming pool and a hot tub. Directly ahead of them were miles of blue ocean. "What do you think?" he asked.

Lila looked at him. She knew it was incredibly expensive, but she wanted it more than anything. It was the perfect house for them. "I love it, but I can understand if it's too much money for us to split," she said.

Bruce brought her hand up to his lips. "I want you to be happy, Lila. If you think about it, nothing's more important than the house we live in. We might have to make sacrifices in order to rent this place. I don't mind vacationing in Bermuda this year instead of Greece, like I had originally planned—just as long as you're happy."

Lila threw her arms around him. "You are *so* romantic." She kissed him passionately.

Mrs. Parker tapped lightly on the glass door, her mouth stretched into a taut smile. "Have we come to any decisions?"

Bruce pulled away from Lila slightly, his hands still clinging to her waist. "Where do we sign?"

"Liz, you're back. I'm so glad to see you," Jessica said cheerfully. "Where did you go?"

Elizabeth looked at her with apprehension. "I

142

finally got up the nerve to get your silk blouse at the dry cleaners. You're not going to be happy, Jess," she said tensely.

Jessica closed her book and reached for the dry-cleaning bag. "What happened?"

Elizabeth lifted the plastic. She pointed to the dark punch stain on the front of the blouse. "They couldn't get the stain out."

Jessica took the bag and hung it on the door-knob of her closet. So much was going on inside her head, a stained blouse was the least of her worries. "Is that all? I thought something serious happened," she said as she slipped on a pair of sandals. "Are you hungry? I'm starved. I thought maybe we could head down to Julio's for a couple of slices."

Elizabeth did a double take. "Did I hear you right? I just told you that I ruined your favorite silk blouse, and now you want to take me out to dinner?"

Jessica ran a brush through her silky hair and threw on a jean jacket. She'd spent the afternoon turning the events of the morning over and over again in her mind. Her feelings for Louis shifted and changed from moment to moment, weaving themselves into a complicated web. Jessica decided that the only way to clear her head was to get off campus. "I suddenly have a craving for the avo-cado, red onion, and black bean pizza Isabella is always talking about." Jessica grabbed the keys to the Jeep. "Don't just stand there with your mouth hanging open. Are you coming?"

Elizabeth laughed. "Sure. Why not?"

Jessica insisted that they take the canvas top off the Jeep. Elizabeth didn't always want to do it. She said it was too much trouble to put back on. But Jessica offered to put it back on herself, if she had to. As far as she was concerned, there was nothing to debate. She needed to drive with the wind in her hair, the open air all around her, the road rolling away beneath them. She wanted to feel like a bird in flight.

"That was a good idea after all," Elizabeth said when they reached the restaurant. "Even though my hair looks like a haystack."

Jessica clipped her sunglasses to the visor of the Jeep. She didn't bother looking in the mirror. "Exhilarating, wasn't it?"

When Jessica needed to escape from the world, there was nothing she liked better than to go somewhere off campus. And Julio's was as good a place as any. It was right near the water, at the end of a midway with carnival rides and an arcade. Jessica loved Julio's red vinyl booths and the smell of oregano mixed with sea salt that wafted through the air. The heaviness that had been pulling her down earlier in the day slowly seemed to evaporate.

It wasn't until they started eating that Elizabeth finally pressed her for answers. "Why have you kept him a secret for so long?"

Jessica hummed happily as she bit into a slice of pizza. "Who?" she asked.

Elizabeth sprinkled red pepper flakes on top of her Greek olive, feta cheese, and tomato pizza. "You know, the new man in your life. You only act like this when you've fallen in love."

Jessica stopped chewing. *Did she say love?* She felt the heaviness threatening to return to her limbs. Was she really in love with Louis? Jessica couldn't be sure. When she'd been driving in the Jeep, with the wind in her hair, Jessica had come to the conclusion that she had taken everything just a bit too seriously. There was still no doubt in her mind that an attraction existed between the two of them. But Jessica decided to simply enjoy it for what it was and not to have any expectations. It didn't have to turn into a relationship. Not if she didn't want it to. "There's no new man in my life," Jessica said, carefully turning the conversation around. "But I have discovered something new and wonderful that I never knew existed."

"What's that?"

"Learning," Jessica said sheepishly. "This Medieval History class has really opened my eyes to a lot of different things."

Elizabeth's eyes bulged. She put down her pizza. "I can't believe those words just came out of my sister's mouth."

"But it's true," Jessica said honestly. With all the studying she had been doing, Jessica was finally beginning to see what it was like to be Elizabeth. "I know I've given you a hard time in the past for studying and doing well in your classes. And I just wanted to say that I'm sorry."

Elizabeth sipped her soda. "All right—apology accepted. Although I'm not so sure there isn't an ulterior motive lurking behind all this."

"There isn't. It's just that I want to be more like you." Jessica winced as she said the words, knowing that she was probably laying it on a little too thick. "I was hoping you could give me a few pointers."

Elizabeth popped an olive into her mouth. "Fire away."

Jessica swirled the ice in her cup with a straw, trying to appear casual. "When there's a dynamic professor who you really find interesting, how do you go about impressing him or her?"

Elizabeth looked at her sister suspiciously. She reached out and touched Jessica's hand. "Is that what this is all about? You're in love with a professor?" she asked.

Jessica looked away. "No—no way," she said emphatically. Her face felt hot. Jessica felt her mouth moving, forming words that had no real connection to her thoughts. "I've just decided that it's time to get serious about my studies. I figure that the best way to start improving my grades is to start impressing my professors."

Elizabeth studied her sister for a moment, and Jessica thought she wasn't buying any of it. "I'll tell you what *not* to do. Don't wear a miniskirt and sit in the front row, or giggle every time the professor makes a joke. They can see through those sorts of things."

"I wouldn't dream of doing anything like that, Liz," Jessica said innocently.

Elizabeth pushed her pizza aside and leaned over the table. "If you're really interested in a professor, Jess, I just want to warn you that it could turn into a messy situation. Be careful."

Jessica shook her head impatiently. "I already told you, I'm not. You're way off base. I just want to know how to get a good grade," she said with indignation.

Jessica stared out the window, watching the faint glow of carnival lights against the night sky. The Ferris wheel turned, a blaze of orange and red. Something about the wheel reminded Jessica of herself. Louis had triggered something that sent her spinning, reeling through space, and yet kept her anchored at the same time. The problem was, she didn't know how to make it stop.

Chapter
Eleven

"Thanks for agreeing to meet with me, Coach Falk," Elizabeth said as she took a seat next to his desk. "I know you have a hectic schedule."

The Sweet Valley University coach smiled. His eyes were kind, instantly making Elizabeth feel at ease. "That's all right, Elizabeth. Todd was one of the best players I've ever had the privilege of coaching at SVU. I'd like to help him in any way I can."

Elizabeth looked around the coach's office. Shelves were lined with trophies, and team photos hung on the walls. Many talented athletes had played at SVU. Elizabeth thought of the hundreds of fans who filled the bleachers at every basketball game to cheer their team on. What if Todd's theory was correct? What if the department *had* paid the recruits? Not only would the other team members be let down, but the fans would also feel betrayed.

"Todd sends you his best. I tried to convince

him to come today, but I think the idea depressed him too much," Elizabeth said sadly.

The coach frowned. "I'm sorry to hear that. If it were up to me, I'd let him back in a heartbeat. Unfortunately the judgment was handed down by a higher power."

"And who was that?" she asked.

"Dr. Beal. When the administration makes a decision, my hands are tied." He leaned back in the chair, his hands folded neatly in front of him.

Elizabeth studied the coach. He did his best to answer her directly, and always looked her in the eye when he spoke. He spoke to her with an ease that gave Elizabeth the sense that he was telling the truth. She was glad to find at least one person in the department she could trust.

He smoothed the front of his blue tie. "This isn't the first time the administration has turned against their own policies," Coach Falk said confidentially. "Between you and me, I've lost some of my best players over the years, all over a few meals, some clothes, and one or two low-interest car loans. They were just a few little perks the administration assured me wouldn't be a problem for me or my players. In hindsight, I guess it wasn't such a good idea."

Elizabeth was puzzled. The administration's own policies seemed to contradict themselves. First they gave the players perks, then they booted them off the team for accepting them. Sports teams always generated a great deal of money for the school. It didn't make sense that they would lure great players to SVU, only to throw them away a few months later. "What about Coach Crane?" she asked. "Isn't he the head of the department? Wouldn't he have some pull with the administration?"

He arched his dark eyebrows thoughtfully. "I suppose so," the coach answered in a low voice. "Can I tell you something off the record?"

Elizabeth leaned forward, anxious to hear what he had to say. "Sure, go ahead."

The coach sat up and stared at her across the desk. "The problem is that Crane's always sided with the administration's decisions."

Elizabeth's spine tingled. A feeling in the pit of her stomach told her that this could be the lead she was looking for. "You mentioned that you gave your star players, like Todd, special privileges. Did those 'privileges' ever include money?"

The coach's eyes narrowed. "I'm afraid I don't know what you're getting at—"

"I'm talking about payoffs," Elizabeth answered bluntly. "To your knowledge, has any player ever been paid to join the SVU basketball team?"

He shook his head. "Absolutely not," the coach answered firmly. "Not in my department."

Elizabeth sighed to herself. Maybe she and Todd had steered themselves in the wrong direction after all. Elizabeth was about to ask the coach if he knew anything about alumni donations when she heard someone enter through the doorway behind her.

"What's going on here?" a voice boomed.

She turned around to see Coach Crane standing there, his face flushed with anger. His eyes looked as if they were going to pop out of his head. "I knew I remembered you from somewhere. You were the one who started all the trouble in the first place." He stared at her with a menacing look that made her shiver. "Ms. Wakefield, I don't know what kind of news station you're running down there, but I suggest you stop chasing ghosts and go after some real news. Maybe sports reporting is too intense for you. Why don't you try something a little less stressful? I'm sure the pottery club could use some press coverage."

I wouldn't be so condescending if I were you, Elizabeth thought as she met his stare. She wanted to jump up from her seat and lunge at him, waving the confidential files under his nose. She would have loved to have seen the reaction on his face when she told him that she knew about the mysterious donations. But she held back. It wasn't time yet. It was better to wait until she had more ammunition. *Then we'll see who's stressed.*

"Let me make one thing clear to you," Coach Crane said, pointing a thick finger at her. "The SVU athletics department has never paid its recruits in the past, and we have no intention of doing so in the future. Now I'm going to ask you to leave."

Elizabeth stood up. "I was finished anyway," she answered coolly. "Thank you for your time, Coach Falk." She shook his hand.

He smiled faintly, and Elizabeth saw a flicker of dread in his eyes. "You're welcome. Please give Todd my best," he said quietly.

Elizabeth left the room with her head held high, not even glancing in Crane's direction. It wasn't until she started to walk down the hallway that her knees felt weak beneath her and her hands began to shake. The full weight of what had just happened suddenly came down on her.

Crane's voice boomed from the basketball office and echoed down the corridor. "If you *ever* talk to that girl again, you're fired!"

"Maybe I should've waited to show you the place after we moved in," Lila said airily as she handed Jessica a tall glass of iced tea. "But I just couldn't wait."

Jessica stretched out on the plush carpeting in front of the stone fireplace. There was no furniture, but it still felt like a great home. "I don't know why you need to move anything in," she said. "This place is great just the way it is."

"It *is* great, isn't it?" Lila said wistfully. "It still needs a few personal touches, though. Bruce hired a team of decorators who will be coming in later this week. It should be fun." She took a sip of iced tea. "How are things at Theta house? Does everyone miss me?"

Jessica dramatically touched her forehead with the back of her hand. "It's only been a day, and Theta house is in shambles. Several of the Thetas have boycotted the mall, and a few have gone on a hunger strike until you return," she said with a smirk.

"How sweet!" Lila laughed. She pointed a long red fingernail in Jessica's direction. "Tell them all that Bruce and I are going to have a huge dinner party for everyone as soon as we're settled."

Jessica's smile dissolved. "Don't tell me you've started cooking. Lila Fowler goes domestic."

Lila's eyes turned up toward the ceiling. "You're so silly sometimes." She giggled. "It's going to be catered, of course."

"Lila!" Bruce called from upstairs. "Lila, come quick, you've got to see this. There's a sauna in the main bathroom!"

Lila squealed and was on her feet in a matter of seconds. "A *sauna*? Looks like I won't have to go to the day spa anymore!" She raced up the stairs.

Jessica laughed and decided to take a stroll out onto the terrace while she waited for Lila to return. As she pushed back the glass doors a blast of warm, salty air hit her. Lila was totally lucky. Not only was she living in a dream house, but she was sharing it with someone who was madly in love with her, even if he happened to have the biggest ego on campus. But even though they'd had their differences in the past, Jessica had to hand it to Bruce— he seemed to be taking good care of Lila. Jessica hoped Lila knew just how fortunate she was.

Jessica leaned against the railing as she watched the waves roll in. She pretended for a moment that the beach house belonged to her, and that she woke up every morning to the beautiful view in front of her. Louis would be there too, drinking his morning coffee before rushing off to teach a class. She would spend her days anxiously waiting for him to return so they could read each other romantic medieval tales by the glow of the firelight.

Jessica groaned. She knew it was an impossible situation, but somehow she couldn't let it go. He was always on her mind. Louis showed her a side of herself that she never knew existed—he opened her eyes to a completely new world. It didn't matter that he was her professor. There was a connection between them that was so strong it couldn't be ignored.

A gentle breeze blew off the Pacific, carrying with it a sweet scent that reminded Jessica of Louis's aftershave. She inhaled deeply. Down the beach she noticed the tall figure of a man, dressed in jeans and a white T-shirt, strolling along the edge of the water. His head was bent low as he walked barefooted in the sand, occasionally skipping rocks into the blue water or stopping to look at shells. It wasn't until he neared the terrace that he lifted his head, and Jessica got a good look at his face.

It was Louis.

Jessica calmly watched him from the terrace, as

if she knew all along that he was going to be there. He looked so young in his casual clothes—Jessica was convinced that he couldn't be more than a few years older than she. On campus he carried himself with confidence and authority, but as she watched him walk along the beach, Jessica sensed an air of sadness around him. He seemed vulnerable.

Should I go talk to him? she wondered. If he was having a rough time, she didn't want to intrude. Then again, maybe he needed someone to talk to. Jessica thought back to the last time they were together, when she read her essay aloud and he leaned so close to her. She'd thought they were going to kiss. She wanted another chance to be alone with him, to see if it could happen. *Don't be stupid,* her mind said. *Elizabeth was right; you have to be careful.* Even though she knew it was best to stay away, Jessica felt a familiar tug pulling against her. It didn't matter what her brain said—she had no choice. She had to follow her heart.

Jessica hurried down the steps toward the beach. "Louis!" she called, running through the soft sand over to where he was standing.

Louis, who was just about to toss a rock into the crashing waves, paused in mid-throw. He looked at her with a mixture of surprise and relief. "Jessica? What are you doing here?" he asked.

He seemed slightly caught off guard, and for a moment Jessica almost regretted calling out to him. The heat of the sun's rays burned her cheeks.

155

"A friend of mine is renting a beach house. I saw you out here, and I thought I'd say hi," she said shyly.

Louis stared at her with an emptiness, as though he were looking right through her. A moment later the spark returned, and a brilliant smile broke over his face. "I'm glad you did," he said.

Jessica turned her head, the sunlight making her hair shine like spun gold. "So what are *you* doing here?" she asked coyly.

"I live down the beach," he said, pointing to a row of houses in the distance. "I thought I'd take a walk and look for a few seashells." He reached into his pocket. "Here's one I found a few yards away."

Jessica touched the glossy surface with her fingertips. The shell was black, with smoky swirls of white, and as smooth and polished as glass. "It's beautiful," she said.

Louis placed the shell gently in the palm of her hand. "You can keep it if you want."

Jessica smiled, her fingers closing over the smooth shell. She thought of the Ferris wheel she saw at Julio's, a blur of light hurling itself through the darkness. "I never would have guessed you were out here collecting shells," she said, holding it tightly. "I figured you were probably watching for Iseult's ship to return."

"What are you in the mood for?" Todd asked Elizabeth as he scanned the snack-bar menu.

Elizabeth picked up a green tray. Her lips twisted into a wry smile as she looked at the trays of doughnuts. She pushed past the sweets and gazed longingly at mounds of onion rings and french fries. "Something salty and loaded with calories."

"That can only mean one thing . . ." Todd said dramatically, reaching for a red-and-white-striped box. "Seasoned curly fries."

Elizabeth's mouth watered. Nothing helped her get through a story block like a dose of junk food. She took a few napkins and a can of cherry soda. "Don't forget the barbecue sauce."

Todd grabbed a handful of barbecue-sauce packets. "What would curly fries be without barbecue sauce? Although I must confess, I've been known to dip them in horseradish sauce every once in a while."

Elizabeth stuck out her tongue. "You've got to be kidding."

"Don't knock it till you try it." Todd paid the cashier.

Elizabeth took a seat near the pool table. "I think I'll pass," she said.

Todd set down the tray and sat in the seat opposite hers. "So tell me more about your meeting with Coach Falk. I can't believe Crane walked into the office and started yelling at you like that."

"You should have seen his face," Elizabeth said, biting into a fry. "He looked like he was going to strangle me."

Todd opened the barbecue-sauce packets,

157

squirting the contents onto a napkin. "He's definitely not the nicest guy I've ever met."

Elizabeth scowled. "You're being generous."

Todd's smile melted into a serious expression. He dipped a potato coil into the sauce. "Thanks for talking to Coach Falk for me. I really appreciate everything you've done."

Elizabeth smiled at him. She was suddenly transported back to high school, when they'd spend their afternoons at the Dairi Burger, chatting over milk shakes. It was nice to be able to share a moment like that with Todd again. Even though she was feeling sentimental, Elizabeth knew that things had changed so much since they'd broken up. They could never go back. "You're welcome. I was glad to help. But I did have a few reasons of my own for going over there."

Todd wiped his fingers on a napkin. "You wanted to get some info about the donations. So what did you find out?"

Elizabeth casually propped her head in her hands, her elbows leaning on the table. "Nothing, really. Coach Falk was adamant that the recruits weren't being paid. And I believe him."

"There's always the possibility that the whole thing could be going on without him knowing," Todd said. "When you're dealing with something illegal like that, I imagine you'd have to go higher to find the culprit. It's the people in power who know how to cover it up."

Elizabeth nodded. "I don't trust Crane at all.

Something tells me that whatever's going on, he's involved." She stared at the flashing lights of the jukebox in the corner. There had to be more to this, something that they were overlooking. "Are you *sure* no one ever offered you money when you were being recruited?"

"Of course I'm sure. That sort of thing would stick in someone's mind," he answered, wiping his mouth with a napkin.

Elizabeth watched as two students grabbed pool cues from the rack on the wall. "But that doesn't mean other people weren't approached," she pointed out. "Were any of the players big spenders?"

Todd's eyes narrowed as if he were deep in thought. "I don't really remember. . . ."

"Was there anyone on the team who was a show-off, flashing money around? What about fancy cars?" she asked. She watched as a short blond guy put quarters into the slot on the side of the pool table. He pushed a button, and the colored balls were released.

"No—I don't think so." Todd rubbed his forehead with his fingertips. Then suddenly his eyes widened.

Elizabeth searched his eyes, looking for clues. "Todd, what is it?"

"I just thought of someone we need talk to."

Chapter Twelve

Louis sighed and dug his toes deep into the cool sand. He was still trying to recover from the shock of seeing Jessica. One moment he was walking along the beach, thinking of her—and the next she was standing beside him, her beautiful hair shining in the sun.

"I'm sorry to say that there is no Iseult in my life," he said softly, knowing it was a lie. In truth, she was standing right next to him, bathed in sunlight, appearing out of nowhere just when he'd needed her. Jessica was a white mast on the horizon.

"I'm sure there must've been someone at one time. . . ." Jessica said, looking down at the shell he had given her.

Painful memories flashed in Louis's mind. *Don't think of her. Just try to forget,* he told himself over and over again. He'd run too far trying to escape the past—he couldn't give into it now. "That was a terrific essay you wrote," Louis said, lightly changing the subject. "I was quite impressed."

"Thanks," Jessica answered shyly. "I'm glad you liked it." She sat down on the beach, tracing circles in the sand with her fingers. "Louis, about what I just said—I'm sorry. I didn't mean to pry."

"No, no—it's all right." He sat down next to her. "I steered you in that direction. Let's forget about it." His eyes were drawn to the soft curve of her lips. Louis wanted to kiss her so badly, it made his insides ache.

Jessica smiled. "How do you like living here?" she asked. Her smile suddenly faded. "That's not too personal a question, is it?"

"Not at all," he answered gently. Louis almost reached out to touch her, but something pulled him back, making him run his fingers through his own hair instead. "I love living here, actually. It's very peaceful." That was another lie. He wanted to tell her the truth, that he was lonely and the solitude made him crazy. He knew she would have understood, she would have cared. But he didn't want to burden her with his problems.

Louis watched Jessica mound sand into a pile, then dig what appeared to be a moat around it. Then she scooped a handful of wet sand and began to sculpt it.

"What are you making?" he asked.

Part of the sculpture toppled over, and Jessica's brow wrinkled in frustration. "It was going to be a sand castle, but it's falling apart on me."

"Let me see." Louis examined the sand castle. "Maybe you're not using enough pressure." He pressed the sand firmly with his hands. "Pretend you're molding clay," he said. He put his arms around Jessica as he showed her how to do it. Her hands felt soft and warm against the gritty, damp sand.

"That does work better," Jessica said. She turned her head, her lips only inches away from his. "But the castle design is pretty sad. Any suggestions?"

Louis tore himself away from her. "What about the Tower of London? That would be fun—but it would take a lot of work."

"That sounds cool!" Jessica said excitedly, knocking over her creation. "Where do we start?"

Louis dug a deep hole, piling the sand next to Jessica. He tried not to notice the perfect shape of her tanned legs. "We'll start from the inside and work out," he said, feeling flustered. "We'll build the White Tower first. That's where the English kings and queens lived before the royals moved to Buckingham Palace."

Jessica cleared an area for the castle to be built on, then piled the wet sand on top of it. "Since you're the expert, I'll build the four walls, and you can do the turrets."

"Sounds good to me," Louis answered. He continued digging in the sand, happy to have a distraction for the afternoon. Earlier, the silence in his house had been unbearable. Louis had felt restless. Then the horrible anxiety started to return, forcing him to go outside. But now, he realized that maybe it was a good thing after all. If he hadn't been driven out, he would have never had this chance to be with Jessica.

"We're running out of mortar . . ." Jessica called, pointing to her diminishing sand pile.

"Sorry." Louis picked up speed. He glanced at Jessica, who was concentrating on making the wall level. Her beautiful eyes seemed to be lost in thought. There was something so innocent about her, it made his heart split wide open. Warmth seemed to flow right out of her, making Louis feel comfortable and safe. He couldn't think of anywhere else in the world that he wanted to be at this very moment. *Nothing can ruin today,* he told himself. *Everything is going to be fine.* Louis smiled with contentment, feeling the tingle of the sunlight on his skin, and he started to relax. He looked down the beach, toward his house.

Suddenly he caught sight of a figure descending the stairs near his patio. Louis stopped digging.

"Ahem." Jessica audibly cleared her throat. "Construction is officially halted."

Louis was frozen in place. Someone was walking slowly and steadily in their direction. Even though it was too far for him to really see, Louis was sure he knew who it was.

It can't be, he thought as the anxiety returned. He had taken so many precautions, been so careful to cover his tracks. He had been sure she wouldn't be able find him this time.

It felt like the air had been sucked out of his lungs as he watched the figure move closer and closer. *Could it really be her?*

"I don't know why I didn't think of Mark Gathers sooner," Todd said to Elizabeth. There was a satisfying *crack* as someone landed a ball in the right corner pocket of the pool table. "After all, we were both punished for accepting preferential treatment. Besides, no one ever did find out where Mark got that brand-new Explorer."

Elizabeth's blue-green eyes were lit with excitement. "Do you know where he is? Can you get in touch with him?"

"I have his number somewhere." Todd sifted through his backpack, looking for his address book. He missed having Mark around; he was the one person who could understand exactly what Todd was going through. Before the scandal broke, Mark had everything going for him—he was a top player with a bright future and he was dating Alexandra Rollins. No one understood what was going through his head when he suddenly picked up and left for L.A.

Todd pulled out a small brown leather book. "Before Mark left SVU, he asked me if I wanted to go with him, to try and make it on my own. At the time I said no, but the more I think about it, I wonder if maybe I should have done it after all."

"Todd, running away isn't the answer." Elizabeth touched his arm consolingly. "There's a

164

good chance that there's more to Mark's story than we realize. Maybe he had other reasons for leaving. But it seems to me that you have too much invested here to throw it all away."

Todd flipped through the book. *Maybe she's right,* he thought. Elizabeth had a way of making things crystal clear. Maybe if he'd left with Mark, he would have had a shot at the pros, but that would also have meant giving up his friends, family, Gin-Yung, and his education. There was too much to lose. He couldn't let the athletics department drive him away that easily. Even though his resolve was starting to break down, Todd preferred to stay and fight.

"Here it is." Todd pulled out a slip of paper from in between the pages. "Let's give him a call."

They went over to the pay phone in the corner of the snack bar, and Todd dialed the number. Elizabeth leaned against the side of the phone. "It's ringing," Todd whispered to her.

Elizabeth crossed her fingers. Todd felt his pulse quickening as he waited for Mark to pick up. Right now, he was their only lead.

"Hello?" a voice said at the other end of the line.

"Hi—Mark?" Todd answered. Elizabeth's face brightened. "This is Todd Wilkins. What's up, buddy?"

"Todd—it's great to hear from you." Mark sounded relaxed and happy. The sound of his voice put Todd at ease. "Things are pretty cool here. Right now I'm selling Lakers T-shirts at the games, but I plan on working my way up. In another year or two, I figure I'll be playing center."

"Sounds great," Todd said with a laugh. "Don't forget us little people when you become famous."

"Of course I won't. How are things at good old SVU?"

Todd rubbed his forehead. "Not so good." He sighed. "They won't let me back on the team."

"Why not?" Mark asked.

"They won't really give me a reason, and I'm not sure why myself."

"That's insane. They can't do that." Mark's voice took on an angry edge. "You were one of the best players that team ever had."

Hearing Mark's words made Todd realize that his anger was justified. He looked at Elizabeth, who was nervously chewing her lip. "There's talk that some of the new recruits might've actually received money, and I think the administration thinks I was one of the people who were paid."

There was silence at the other end.

Todd glanced meaningfully at Elizabeth. He continued talking into the phone. "I don't think there's any truth to the rumor—I didn't know anyone who was paid." Elizabeth moved closer. It seemed she was trying to hear Mark's voice through the receiver. "Did you know anyone?" Todd asked.

"No, I didn't," he answered abruptly.

Todd paused. "Did anyone try to give you money?"

"No way," Mark protested. "You're talking about something totally illegal. If someone offered me money, I would've been out of there long ago."

Todd shook his head, and Elizabeth moved away. "Me too. Privileges are one thing; money is a whole different story."

"I can't believe they're treating you like that," Mark said. "You deserve better. Why don't you leave that crummy place and come to L.A.? I could get you some work—there's an opening at the concessions stand."

"Selling hot dogs to hungry Lakers fans is tempting," Todd said jokingly. "But I'm going to have to pass this time around."

"Let me know if you change your mind," Mark said. "Keep in touch."

"I will." Todd hung up the phone.

Elizabeth looked at him. "I guess we struck out."

Todd nodded. "I know Mark, and judging from the way he reacted, I know he was being straight with me."

Elizabeth leaned against the wall. "So where does this lead us now?" she asked.

Todd sighed. "To a dead end."

"Professor Miles, are you all right?" Jessica asked as she watched him stare into the distance. "What's wrong?"

Louis looked at her. The light in his green eyes seemed to be flickering out. "Nothing," he said distractedly.

He finished the last turret on the White Tower, and Jessica looked at it proudly. Their sand castle was a work of art.

"What's next?" Jessica asked, scooping out more sand from the hole. "Are there any more buildings we need to make?"

Louis looked up again, his eyes focused somewhere in the distance. "We can add the other buildings later. . . . Why don't you start working on the outer wall." He began carving windows and doorways with a small stick.

Jessica worked with enthusiasm, molding the sand the exact way Louis had showed her. She'd loved the way his hands had covered hers. He had a wonderful, gentle touch. Suddenly she remembered Lila. Did she even realize that Jessica had disappeared? Jessica wondered if she should go back to the house and tell her where she was, but she quickly dismissed the thought. She didn't want anything to ruin this perfect moment with Louis.

"How long have you been in Sweet Valley?" Jessica asked, filling the silence that had fallen between them.

Louis continued working as though he didn't hear her. "I'm sorry," he said a moment later. "Did you say something?"

Lines appeared on his forehead and around his mouth. *Why is he acting so odd all of a sudden?* Jessica wondered. He seemed to be slipping into himself, like a frightened turtle.

"How long have you been here?" she asked again, hoping to coax him out of his shell.

"A little while . . ." he answered vaguely. He turned away and stared into the distance, his eyes blank, expressionless.

Jessica added more sand to the wall to make it thicker. Her eyes traced the smooth line of his square jaw. "What made you decide to come here?" she persisted.

"All sorts of reasons," he snapped.

Jessica looked at him, stunned. He had never spoken to her like that before. Louis's eyes were fixed on a point farther down the beach. Jessica saw the figure of a woman slowly approaching them from several yards away.

Jessica swallowed hard. "Do you know her?"

Louis suddenly stood up. "I'd rather not discuss my private life if you don't mind," he said curtly. He brushed the sand off his jeans. "That wall looks pretty good. All you have to do is surround the White Tower, dig a moat, and then you'll be done," he said, spouting off the directions to her as if he were speaking to a toddler. His jaw was set. "I'll see you in class, Jessica." He walked away.

Jessica cringed at his stinging words as if she'd been bitten by a poisonous snake. Hot tears sprang to her eyes. In one swift motion she crushed the crumbling castle wall with her fist.

Winston propped his feet on a library chair and

169

tried to make sense of the physics problem he was working on. He had been working on the same problem for almost an hour, calculating and recalculating but coming up with a different answer each time. His back was beginning to ache from sitting on the hard wooden chair for so long.

The library was completely quiet, except for the sound of pages being turned and pens scratching notebook paper. The silence was pressing down on Winston, making him feel like a caged rat. He tapped his pencil compulsively on the cover of his book. Winston thought of taking a study break to visit Denise, but he knew it would be a waste of time—she didn't want to see him. The only thing left to do was to stay right where he was and study.

"Fine," Winston said aloud, his voice slicing through the stillness. He wrote out a series of calculations onto his paper, trying to make it look official. It didn't matter if the answer wasn't correct; all that mattered was that Professor Stark saw he was making an effort. Then he'd help him study for the test.

Winston sat back, whistling a tune, and examined his work. He'd only managed to finish two problems and read five pages in the three hours he'd been in the library. But it wasn't entirely his fault. The place was too quiet to get any real work done; plus his mind kept wandering back to Denise.

Winston laid his head on his book to rest his

eyes for a minute. *Get a grip,* he told himself. *You'll see her in a few days—as soon as this exam is over.* No matter how rational his mind was, Winston's heart felt differently. Everything he came in contact with reminded him of Denise. He took a deep breath. Even the smell of the ink from the pages of his textbook reminded him of her perfume.

Wait a minute . . . The scent of Denise's perfume became stronger. Winston opened one eye. Denise and a few of her sorority sisters walked by his table and sat in a semicircle of upholstered chairs near the window. He blinked a few times to make sure she was real.

Winston suddenly bolted upright. "Denise!" he whispered loudly. Denise sat back in the chair and opened a book in her lap, apparently settling in for a study session. Her hair was pulled back in a blue bandanna. She didn't seem to hear Winston calling to her.

"Denise!" Winston said again, a little louder this time. He stared intently at her, ignoring glares from the students in the study carrels next to him. It was a relief just to see her face again. "Denise!"

Denise looked up for a moment, then spotted Winston. She smiled broadly at him, then waved before returning to her reading.

Winston waited for her to look up again, but she didn't move. He felt as if a giant fist had reached down and squeezed his heart. "Denise!" Winston said, nearly shouting.

"Why don't you go over and talk to her?" an angry student hissed. A few others nodded.

"Good idea," Winston answered, leaping to his feet. He wasn't going spend all of his time waiting for her—he had to take control of the situation. He walked over and stood by her chair.

Denise looked up at him. "Hey, Win—how's the studying going?" she whispered.

Winston squatted beside her. The smell of her perfume made his head fuzzy. "How come you haven't answered my calls? I've left you a ton of messages."

"I know you have."

"Are you mad at me?" he asked sullenly.

Denise giggled. "Of course not."

Winston touched her hand. He'd almost forgotten what it was like to be near her. "Then why are you doing this? You're driving me crazy."

Denise closed her book. "I'm not trying to be mean," she said, turning to face him. "You said you can't study when I'm around, that I should stay away until after your exam. I'm just doing what you wanted."

He shook his head. "I didn't mean it that way," Winston said. "I didn't say you had to stay away *altogether*. We could at least meet for dinner or something. Why don't we have dinner together tonight?"

Denise smiled patiently. "Win, get back to your studying. You need as little distraction as possible right now."

172

"That's the whole problem." Winston's pitch rose two notches. "I can't get any work done if I don't see you. I think about you all the time."

"That's so sweet." Denise gave him a dry peck on the cheek. "Now go back over there and I'll see you in a few days," she said, waving him away.

Winston trudged slowly back to his table, his shoulders slumped. He tried to focus on his work but ended up just staring at Denise the whole time. Winston was waiting to see if she would turn her head, but Denise didn't look in his direction. Not even once.

Chapter
Thirteen

"Are you all right, Jess?" Elizabeth asked. Jessica was curled up on her bed, staring blankly at the wall of their room. While it was unusual to see her sister like this, Elizabeth wasn't entirely surprised. Her sister had been doing many strange things lately. "Do you need anything?" she asked.

"I'm fine, thanks," Jessica said absently. "I guess I'm just a little tired." The phone rang, and Jessica suddenly sprang to life, leaping for the phone. "Hello?" she said into the receiver. Her face fell. "It's lover boy," she said, handing the phone to Elizabeth.

Elizabeth reached for the phone excitedly—there was so much she wanted to tell Tom. It felt as if he'd been away for years. "Hi, Tom—how's Vegas?"

"Amazing," Tom said energetically. Just from the sound of his voice, Elizabeth knew he was having a great time. "They're treating us like royalty. But it's been incredibly busy. There are tons of meetings and seminars to go to. Craig Maser arrived this afternoon, so there's going to be a party for him tonight. I haven't even had a chance to start preparing the copy for my broadcast."

Elizabeth sat down on her perfectly made bed. "Did you have a chance to meet with Angela Hunter yet?"

"Several times," Tom said casually. "She's following Craig Maser's story pretty closely, so she's been asking me to help her with the details. She's a terrific woman."

Elizabeth ignored the pang of envy that seized her. "That's great. You'll have to tell me all about her when you get back." She twirled the telephone cord around her fingers. "Any other interesting things happen?"

"Too many to tell," Tom said. "I wish you were here, Liz. I really miss you."

Elizabeth started to melt. "I miss you too. I can't wait for you to come back here so things can get back to normal."

"Is everything okay at the station?" he asked.

Elizabeth smiled to herself. Tom might be rubbing elbows with professional journalists, but she was starting to come into her own right here at SVU. "There *have* been a few intriguing developments . . ." she said mysteriously. Her spine began to tingle with excitement. "I started working on the alumni donations piece, and you won't believe what I found."

"What?"

Elizabeth looked at Jessica, who was drifting off to sleep. "I won't go into the details right now, but it seems that there have been several large donations to the athletics department in the last few years. But as far as I can tell, the money isn't going into the department. I talked to Coach Crane, and he's obviously hiding something. Todd and I think the money is going to pay new recruits."

"Wait a minute," Tom said, sounding irritated. "What does Todd have to do with this?"

"I grilled him about what he knew—I thought someone might have approached him when he was on the team," she answered defensively. "He's my connection to the athletics program."

"Look, Liz, don't do anything else," Tom said firmly. "Wait until I get back."

"Why? We're getting so close—"

"If you're right about this, it could be really big," Tom argued. "We need to make sure it's handled properly."

Elizabeth felt her temperature rising. "What makes you think Todd and I can't handle it?" she asked hotly.

Tom lowered his voice. "Don't get upset. I just think maybe this story should be left to someone with a little more expertise."

Elizabeth squeezed her fingers tightly around the receiver. *Did he just call me an amateur?* She felt as though she were about to explode. "Listen, Tom—you gave me this assignment because it was busywork that you didn't have time for. Now that it's turned into a real story, you're telling me I'm too unseasoned to handle it. You're not making any sense."

"I can't believe you don't see what's going on here, Liz. I'm hundreds of miles away, and it's crystal clear to me," Tom said bitterly. "Todd is obviously lying. He's trying to manipulate you into helping him back on the team. Stay away from him. When I get back, I'm going to have a talk with that guy."

"*That guy* happens to be a good friend of mine." Elizabeth seethed. Jessica's eyes blinked open. "I'm not an idiot who can't tell when she's being manipulated. Give me some credit, Tom."

"I'm not trying to upset you. I just want you to be aware of what's going on."

Elizabeth's knuckles were white as she gripped the phone. "I can handle myself just fine."

A deafening silence hung in the air. After a moment, Tom spoke. "I'd better go; I have a meeting in five minutes," he said quietly. "I'll call you again soon."

Elizabeth said good-bye, then slowly set down the phone. She hated to break the phone connection—so much between them was still unresolved. Her stomach was being pressed into a tight ball of conflicting emotions. How could she love him so much and be so angry with him at the same time?

"Trouble in paradise?" Jessica asked dryly.

Elizabeth paced the floor, talking aloud to herself.

177

"He thinks I'm some sort of naive idiot who can't handle a story by herself . . . I'll show him. I'll crack open the entire investigation before he comes back." Angela Hunter wouldn't give up an investigation just because her boyfriend asked her to, and Elizabeth wasn't about to either. In fact, she was more determined than ever to get to the bottom of it all.

"Don't you hate it when they treat you like you're two years old?" Jessica rolled over lazily. "Is there anything I can do to help?"

"I don't know; maybe," Elizabeth mumbled. She thought about the dead end she and Todd had suddenly reached when Mark Gathers didn't have any information. But Mark couldn't be their only lead. There had to be tons of other players she could get in touch with. "Jess, you were friends with some of the guys on the basketball team, right?"

"Sure, I know a few of them. Why?"

Elizabeth crossed her arms in front of her. "Who were you friends with?"

"There was Dexter Robinson . . . Tim Mathews . . . and Daryl Cartright." Jessica counted them off on her fingers.

Elizabeth wrote down the names on a piece of paper. "Are they still here on campus? Do you think you could help me set up an interview with them?"

Jessica shrugged. "Dex and Tim aren't a problem, but Daryl isn't here anymore. He left school after getting kicked off the team," she said.

Elizabeth stopped. "Why was he kicked off the team?"

Jessica yawned. "Don't you remember Daryl? He was really tall and skinny and had bright red hair. At the beginning of the year, there was this big deal about him being the next SVU star."

Elizabeth scratched her head. The details were coming back to her in a haze. "If I remember right, they kicked him off the team after the fourth game, but I don't remember why."

Jessica sat up. "It was because he suddenly became a mediocre shooter. They counted on him to be the lead scorer, but suddenly he wasn't getting the baskets."

He was the one. Elizabeth knew it. He would be her link to solving the mystery. She had to talk to him right away. "After he left school, where did he go?"

Jessica shook her head. "I don't have a clue."

"I've asked you both to meet me here today because Bruce and I are having a bit of a crisis." Lila's voice rose above the chatter of the coffee-house. She took a delicate sip of her café au lait. "I need your help."

Jessica and Isabella exchanged sideways glances. "What's wrong?" Jessica asked.

Lila pushed the coffee cups and the narrow vase of daisies to one side, then stacked several books and folders on the small wooden table. She opened the books one by one, revealing bright swatches of cloth and room diagrams. "This is the problem," she said.

Isabella's long, slender fingers touched the cloth samples. "Having trouble picking out the right floral prints for your living-room pillows?"

"Oh, I wish it were as simple as that. . . ." Lila shook her head tiredly, as if someone had just asked her to redecorate the White House. "Pillows are just the beginning."

Jessica pushed in her chair to let the waitress by. Her eyes glossed over the endless pages of room layouts. "I thought the interior decorators were going to take care of all this for you."

Lila looked at Jessica in a way that suggested she had a lot to learn about moving into a fashionable new home. "Just because you hire decorators doesn't mean you can give them free rein to do whatever they want." Lila waved her arms in a broad gesture. "There are still so many things we have to decide on. We asked them to come up with a few different motifs to start."

Isabella played with the ribbon choker hanging from her elegant neck. "And what did they come up with?"

Lila pulled out a portfolio from the file. "Bruce and I narrowed it down to two different styles. The problem is I like one of them and he likes the other." She spread out the contents of the folder. "This is the one I like."

Jessica leafed through the photographs of elegant mahogany tables and rich floral fabrics. The style was very elaborate, but seemed to suit Lila's personality perfectly. "This is beautiful. I love French country," she said.

Lila beamed. She pointed to the decorations she liked the most. "And the pillows even come with silk tassels. I think it would look gorgeous." She then opened a folder marked *Bruce*. Lila made a face as if she had just swallowed bitter medicine. She laid out the photographs. "This is what I'm up against."

Jessica tried to suppress a giggle, and Isabella gave her a knowing look. Spread out on the table was a collection of animal prints. There were photos of zebra curtains, leopard-print couches, big clay pots with artificial trees. According to Bruce's diagram, a bearskin rug would go in front of the fireplace.

"A jungle theme can be exciting too," Isabella said, choking back a laugh. "You can go on safari without leaving the comforts of home."

Lila gritted her teeth. "I'm not putting a dead animal in front of my fireplace."

Someone turned on the stereo, and the cool sounds of John Coltrane's saxophone filled the coffeehouse. Jessica took a bite of biscotti. "Why don't you two compromise? You could mix the two motifs together. Two continents in one house."

Lila considered her point. "But wouldn't it be just a bit tacky to have a carved elephant tusk next to the silver candlesticks?"

"You could always have one theme on the

ground floor and then a different one upstairs," Isabella added, tapping her fingers in time to the music.

"Some of this jungle stuff isn't so bad," Jessica said, looking at the pictures. "Like this mosquito-net bed. It has an iron frame and then this gauzy material is draped over it. It looks like an exotic canopy."

"That *is* kind of cool," Lila said, examining the picture again.

"You could keep the French country for the main areas, but keep the jungle theme just for the upstairs. I think it would be fun," Jessica said.

"Maybe I should hire *you* to do the decorating," Lila said. "On second thought, you probably wouldn't get any work done. I'd find you out on the beach building sand castles like you did last time."

Jessica's face fell. She had been trying to forget about earlier that day, when Louis had stormed off. But now the memories came flooding back. The more she thought about it, the more convinced Jessica was that it was all her fault. Louis left because she had asked too many personal questions. If only she hadn't gone to talk to him in the first place, none of this would have happened.

Isabella nodded. "I think Jessica's right. You need to compromise or there could be problems between you two later on."

Lila tucked the samples back into the folders. "Thank you both. You just saved our relationship."

No problem, Jessica thought ruefully. Solving other people's romantic problems was a piece of cake. Solving her own was a completely different story.

A stylishly dressed receptionist stood in the entrance of the waiting room, waving at Elizabeth. "Dr. Beal will see you now," she said.

Elizabeth followed her down the hallway through the maze of administrative offices. She imagined what Tom would say if he knew she was on her way to plead Todd's case to the head of the administration. Her pulse quickened when she remembered how he'd suggested that Todd was only using her to get what he wanted. But Tom's words had the opposite effect on Elizabeth. Now she was more determined than ever to get Todd back on the team.

The receptionist smiled at her as she opened the door to a large office. Elizabeth looked inside to see a bald man with a mustache seated behind a desk. "Dr. Beal, this is Elizabeth Wakefield," the receptionist said to him.

"Good morning, Ms. Wakefield," he said. His voice sounded like gravel, but it was friendly.

"Good morning, Dr. Beal," Elizabeth said in her most polite tone. "I'm here on behalf of my close friend, Todd Wilkins." She sat down on a soft leather chair. His desk was made of solid wood, and an abstract painting hung on the wall behind the desk.

"I'm familiar with Mr. Wilkins's case," Dr. Beal said. "Is it safe to say that you are here to ask that the administration reverse its decision?"

"Yes," Elizabeth said candidly. "Todd has been punished, and he's very sorry for what he did. He's a wonderful person and a great athlete. I think it would be a great loss to the SVU team not to let him play."

Dr. Beal smoothed the lapels of his expensive suit. "I sympathize with Mr. Wilkins, but you must understand that this sort of scandal generates damaging publicity for the school. Not only will it prevent potential students from applying here, but we also stand to lose important alumni support." He put his hands together, only the tips of his fingers touching. "The relationship between SVU and its alumni has deteriorated in the last few years, due to policy changes that the alums don't care for. We've lost millions of dollars in financial backing from many powerful alumni. I've been working hard to restore the relationship so that SVU can regain some of its funding. As much as I'd like to help Mr. Wilkins, I feel compelled to make an example out of him to show the Alumni Association that we are running a clean sports program."

Elizabeth's eyes narrowed. It was strange that an outside group could have so much influence. "So are you telling me that all your decisions are based on how the Alumni Association will react?"

"Not all the decisions," Dr. Beal said. "But in this particular case, you're correct."

This can't be it, Elizabeth thought. *There must be someone else I can talk to.* She looked directly at Dr. Beal, her voice unwavering. "What if I pleaded Todd's case before the association and they agreed that he should be allowed back on the team? *Then* would you reverse your decision?"

"I would certainly consider it." Dr. Beal flipped through his address file. "The person you should speak with is Mr. T. Clay Santos. He's the head of the Alumni Association. Here's his address." He handed the card to her.

Elizabeth copied the address and gave him back the card. "Thank you, Dr. Beal. I hope to be in touch with you soon."

The phone rang. "Good luck," he called to her as he picked it up.

Elizabeth walked out of his office, holding Mr. T. Santos's number in her hand. Getting information was a wild-goose chase. Everyone passed her off to someone else. She hoped that setting up a meeting with the Alumni Association would be the last stop before Todd was reinstated on the team.

Elizabeth heard Dr. Beal talking on the phone. "Yes, sir," he said, his voice suddenly sounding nervous. "She just left my office."

Elizabeth stopped in her tracks, listening outside the door. "Please calm down, sir. I didn't tell her anything," Dr. Beal said. The person at the other end of the line was obviously very upset. "Don't worry, I will do everything necessary . . . thank you, sir."

Elizabeth heard him hang up the phone.

*　　*　　*

"I love old movies," Gin-Yung said, popping a tape into the VCR. She slipped off her penny loafers and curled up beside Todd on his couch.

"Alone at last . . ." Todd said, putting his arm around her. He had been so busy lately, trying to get back on the team and helping Elizabeth with her case, that he and Gin-Yung hadn't had a quiet moment together in several days. Todd reached down to kiss her, when suddenly the phone rang. "I'm sorry," he said. "Don't move." He got up to answer it.

"Yeah?" he said into the receiver.

"Todd, this is Elizabeth—"

"Hi, Liz," he said, looking at Gin-Yung. "What's up?"

"I just spoke with Dr. Beal. He said that there was nothing he could do about your situation. Apparently he's too worried about how it would look to the Alumni Association. But I managed to set up a meeting tomorrow night with the head of the association, to hear your case. If the association sympathizes with you, there's a good chance that Dr. Beal will too."

"That's great news! Thanks so much," Todd said excitedly. "You've really come through for me."

"Anything for an old friend," Elizabeth answered. "We have to be at the meeting at eight. Meet me in the student parking lot at around seven thirty."

"I'll see you then." Todd hung up the phone

and immediately went to his closet. He pulled out a white dress shirt and a dark suit.

"What was that about?" Gin-Yung asked, turning down the volume on the television.

"Liz got me an interview with the head of the Alumni Association. She thinks they have enough pull to get me back on the team." He grabbed a handful of neckties and draped them one by one over his suit. "I have to meet her tomorrow night at seven thirty."

"That's great!" Gin-Yung said. She watched as he tore through his closet. "But aren't you getting ready just a tad early?"

Todd shook his head. "I want to make sure everything is ready to go," he answered. "I don't want to take anything for granted."

"Wear the paisley tie—stylish, but conservative." She clicked off the television. "What should I wear?"

Todd plugged in his iron. "For what?" he asked distractedly.

Gin-Yung rolled her eyes. "For the meeting. I'm going with you, of course. You need moral support."

Todd sighed as he examined his dress shoes for scuff marks. "I'm glad you want to come," he said, approaching the subject delicately. "But I think it would be better if you stayed here. I think the committee would be more sympathetic to me if I presented my case alone."

Gin-Yung toyed with the hem of her khaki

pants. "Elizabeth is going to be with you."

Todd's tongue felt like it was three feet thick. He couldn't explain it himself. How could he possibly make her understand? "She's only going to be there because it involves a story she's working on. I can't get into it now, because it might jeopardize her story."

"I'm a sportswriter, in case you've forgotten," Gin-Yung said angrily.

Todd laid out his shirt on his desk and started to iron. He didn't want to get into this argument. He'd just found out that he had a shot at getting back on the team, and now he had to battle it out with Gin-Yung over something stupid. "Then you understand the bind I'm in. It's her story, not mine—I don't have a right to talk about it."

"There's more to it than that." Gin-Yung's dark eyes looked sad. "Todd, I think we need to talk."

Todd put down the iron and took a seat next to her. Why did this have to be so complicated?

Gin-Yung took his hand in hers. "I need to know where this is headed—where things stand between us. I was under the impression that we were going to make a commitment to each other."

Todd touched her reassuringly. "We are. That's what I want."

"But that's not what you're doing," she argued. "Making a commitment means letting that person into your life. I like Elizabeth, but you've been sharing so much with her lately, and I'm suddenly feeling left out."

Todd smoothed back her silky hair. "It's not like that, really. I want us to be together."

"Then tell me what's going on."

Todd was cornered. He had a feeling that the answer to the mysterious donations was within their grasp; all they needed were a few more days and they could crack it. He put his arm around her. "Just wait a little longer and you'll know everything. I promise."

Gin-Yung pulled away from him. "Todd, I don't how much longer I can wait."

Chapter Fourteen

"Today we are going to talk about the legends of King Arthur," Louis said, leaning against the edge of his desk. "But before we start, does anyone have any questions about our last lecture?"

Jessica slumped down in her seat in the back of the room. She had a million questions she wanted to ask him, but none of them had anything to do with medieval history.

Louis looked around the room. No hands were raised. "In that case, let's begin."

Jessica looked down to the front of the room. In the front-row chair that she usually sat in was a short girl with dark hair that Jessica didn't know. Louis looked at the student and smiled, as if nothing were unusual. The girl smiled back. *Am I that easily replaced?* Jessica wondered. A cloud of jealousy hung over her. How could he carry on as if nothing was wrong when she was dying inside?

A girl with wavy auburn hair and freckles leaned toward Jessica and whispered in her ear, "Is it just me, or is Professor Miles looking really hunky today?"

Jessica tugged the corners of her mouth up into a twisted smile. He did look good. He wasn't wearing his usual tweed jacket, only dress pants and a dark blue turtleneck. The sleeves were pushed up to his elbows, showing the tanned skin of his forearms. It was the tan he probably got the day they were building the sand castle on the beach.

The girl leaned over again. "Do you think he has a girlfriend?" she asked.

Jessica gave her a smug grin. "I know he does," she lied.

"What's her name?" the girl asked.

"Jessica?" Louis called out.

Did he just call my name, or did I imagine that? Jessica looked up to the front. His eyes were fixed her. "Yes?" she answered softly.

Louis was pointing to a time line he had drawn on the chalkboard. "Do you know the answer?" he asked. He looked at her with cool detachment, as if he were asking a stranger for directions.

Jessica swallowed the panic that was rising in her throat. "I-I'm sorry," she stammered. "I didn't hear the question."

Louis looked away and addressed the entire classroom. "Does anyone know the answer?"

"I do," said the girl with the auburn hair.

Jessica felt burning tears of humiliation welling up in her eyes. She hated the impersonal way he'd spoken to her, then passed over her so easily. *If only I hadn't ruined everything,* she thought. Obviously the questions she had asked him had suddenly changed his mind about her. She didn't stand a chance with so many girls eager to take her place. Jessica wished she could drop out of the class or even transfer to another school. Seeing Louis for the rest of the semester would be unbearable.

I've got to make it up to him. Jessica tore a sheet of paper out of her notebook. Maybe the only thing left to do was to write him a letter. She'd explain that she was sorry she'd asked so many personal questions at the beach. She'd tell him that she had crossed the line—taken liberties. Maybe it wouldn't change anything between them, but at least she wouldn't have to spend the rest of the term feeling completely humiliated.

Jessica reached into her bag and pulled out the shell he had given her. Its smooth surface filled her with longing. She wrote furiously, holding the shell as she wrote.

Dear Professor Miles—

> *Thank you for the shell you gave me and for helping me build the sand castle. I had a wonderful time. I hope my questions didn't offend you, though I have a feeling they did. I only asked them because I wanted to know*

*more about you. But it was none of my busi-
ness. And I know that now. I didn't mean to
pry, and I'm sorry. I hope you'll forgive me,
and that we can continue to be friends. I
really treasure what we have.*

*Sincerely,
Jessica Wakefield*

Jessica read the note over several times. It was straightforward and not too emotional. The only part she wasn't sure of was the last line—the part about treasuring their relationship. She hoped she wasn't being too pushy, but she felt it needed to be said. There was something special between them, and she wanted to acknowledge it. Jessica took a deep breath, feeling as if a burden had been lifted.

When class ended, Jessica walked down the center aisle toward the front desk. Louis was turned around, erasing the chalkboard. Her plan was to slip the note into his briefcase when he wasn't looking. But when she got there, she couldn't do it. The briefcase was right there, open in front of her, and he was looking away. Still she couldn't bring herself to do it. She was too afraid of how he'd react.

Jessica turned around and headed for the door, shoving the note into her pocket. Her fingers clutched the shell tighter, its rough edges cutting deeper into the palm of her hand.

*　　　*　　　*

Todd rushed out of his dorm into the dark night. He was already ten minutes late. Elizabeth was probably on time as usual, waiting for him in the parking lot. If everything went smoothly, they'd make it to their meeting with Mr. Santos at exactly eight.

It had rained earlier, and the sky was still cloudy, covering the stars. The moon looked as if it had melted, a dull circle of light shining through the clouds. Todd jogged along the path, mentally taking inventory to make sure he had everything he needed. His clothes were in perfect order, and he was carrying a leather briefcase with all the documents he would need to prove his case. He laughed as he heard the squeak of his dress shoes with each step. He felt more like a stockbroker than a college basketball player.

Maybe I should have let Gin-Yung come to the meeting after all, he thought as he slowed his pace. He didn't mean to hurt her feelings—he was only thinking about himself at the time. He'd tried to convince her that it was because of Elizabeth's story, which was partially true, but it was mostly because he was too embarrassed. He didn't want Gin-Yung to hear him retell the events of the scandal or see him groveling for forgiveness. He was afraid she'd think less of him.

Todd tried to imagine how it all looked from her point of view. He knew it must have seemed odd to her that he was spending so much time with his ex-girlfriend. He wished he could have told her about the case, about his feelings; maybe she would have understood. He should've at least reassured her that he and Elizabeth weren't getting back together. He wished he could tell her right now.

A thick cloud passed over the moon, covering it completely. Todd walked in between two rows of hedges that lined the path. *As soon as this is over, you can tell her everything,* he said to himself. *Right now, you have to concentrate on your future.* The thought of his future sent shivers down his spine. It terrified him to think what would happen if the Alumni Association didn't take his side. Instantly the full impact of the meeting he was about to have with Mr. Santos hit him. It weighed down on him like a stack of bricks. This was his last chance to clear his name.

Think positive, Todd repeated to himself as he walked down the dark path. He had every right to be back on that team, and he was going to do whatever he had to in order to make it happen.

"Hey—" Todd called out in surprise. Two large men dressed all in black had jumped from behind the bushes directly in front of him. One of the men punched Todd squarely in the stomach. It happened so quickly, he didn't have time to react.

Todd sank to his knees, trying to catch his breath. "Who . . . who are you?" he said hoarsely. He lifted his head slightly to look at his attackers.

The man who'd punched him pushed Todd's

head down forcefully. "Don't look up if you know what's good for you," his raspy voice said.

"Why are you doing this? What do you want?" Todd clutched his stomach. It felt like a giant fireball was searing his insides. "Please don't hurt me. . . ."

"Just shut up and we'll tell you all you need to know," the voice hissed like a serpent. "We've heard that you've been sticking your nose where it doesn't belong. You've been snooping around in other people's personal files."

"I haven't done anything. . . ." Todd muttered. The man who was holding his face down gave a sharp kick into Todd's ribs. Todd cried out as the white-hot pain shot through his body.

"Don't deny it. You'll only make things worse for yourself," the voice said. "Just keep your nose clean, and everything will be fine. But if you don't . . ."

Todd gritted his teeth, gathering all the strength he had left. He jumped up suddenly, throwing off the man who was standing over him. Todd turned to run, but the soles of his dress shoes slipped in the fresh mud. He fell awkwardly to the ground.

The two men were on him in a matter of seconds. One pinned Todd's arms at his sides while the other punched him squarely in the face. Todd felt the warm, sticky ooze of blood flowing from his nose. A painful throb pounded in his lower lip.

The men stood up, leaving Todd moaning in

the dirt. "Consider this a warning," the raspy voice said menacingly. "And tell your little reporter friend that she'd better mind her own business too, or she's going to be in more trouble than she ever imagined."

Where is he? Elizabeth wondered as she waited for Todd in the parking lot. The moon kept disappearing behind the clouds, making it a particularly dark night.

Elizabeth tapped her foot impatiently. She'd rallied hard to get Mr. Santos to schedule a meeting so soon to hear Todd's case. They already had enough things against them—the last thing they needed was to show up late.

Elizabeth leaned against the large rock that marked the entrance to the parking lot, careful not to wrinkle her beige linen suit. She wished she'd remembered to tell Todd where she parked—then she could be waiting in the comfort of her Jeep. But instead she had to wait for him at the entrance, so he wouldn't waste time looking for the Jeep among the hundreds of cars in the lot.

Hurry, Todd. Elizabeth didn't like empty parking lots, especially on such a dark night. There was something about the quietness, the isolation, that always made her feel panicky. *Just relax,* she told her heart as it started to race. *He'll be here any minute.*

She nervously glanced at her watch. It was five minutes to eight. There was no way around it;

197

they were going to be at least twenty minutes late now. Normally Todd was so punctual. *What's keeping him?*

Suddenly Elizabeth felt the tiny hairs on the back of her neck stand up, as if someone were watching her. She swore she could hear the faint crunch of shoes on gravel, coming up from behind. She swallowed hard, then slowly turned to look around. The sound stopped. She didn't see anyone.

It was probably all in her mind, but Elizabeth wasn't about to take any chances. She stood up and quickly walked across the road onto the path leading back to campus.

Elizabeth's body tensed. What if Todd was backing out on her? The thought made her shake with anger. She had gone through too much trouble for him to back out now. He was going to be there, whether he wanted to or not. Elizabeth was going to see this through to the end. First she'd locate Todd. Then she'd call Mr. Santos to tell him they were going to be a little late.

"Don't forget to lock the outside door," Professor Stark said as he collected his papers. "I think everyone has left for the night."

"I won't forget," Louis answered. "Have a good night."

Professor Stark shuffled out the door. Louis continued to correct the essays his students had turned in. It didn't bother him at all to stay so late—in fact, he liked it. He even liked the cramped, confined office he shared with Professor Stark. It was better than the wide-open space of his empty house. Sometimes Louis would work until the wee hours of the morning, even falling asleep at his desk on occasion, just to avoid having to go back home.

Louis wrote a few comments in the margin of a student's paper, then put it in the C-grade pile. He was disappointed with how the essays had turned out in general. There were many more C and D papers than B's and A's. It made him wonder if he was at fault. *Maybe I'm not getting through to them,* he thought with frustration. He reached for the next essay to be corrected. It was written by Jessica Wakefield.

Louis read the essay, even though she had already read it to him aloud in class. He heard her voice reading each word, slowly and deliberately, remembering how sweet it had sounded. She'd looked so beautiful and so fragile at the same time, like the shell he had given her at the beach. In those few moments he'd felt more happiness than he had felt in an entire year.

Louis closed his eyes and tried to imagine how it would feel to kiss Jessica. The thought of not being able to do so filled him with a wrenching pain. *Why does she have this effect on me?* he wondered. After all, she was one of his students. In the past Louis had never even come close to crossing the invisible line that was drawn between teacher and student. Until he met Jessica.

Louis thought back to the last class, when Jessica was hiding herself in the back row. She looked so upset, and he had a feeling it had something to do with the way he'd acted on the beach. He had wanted to stop the class to tell her how sorry he was about the way he had treated her, to tell her that she didn't do anything wrong. He wanted to pull her aside at the end of class, but he was too embarrassed to tell her how he felt. Maybe it was better to leave it this way, with her keeping a distance. As much as it hurt, he couldn't let himself become involved with her. It just wasn't right.

Louis heard the faint, tapping sound of footsteps in the hallway. Stark had said the building was empty. He was suddenly alert, listening very closely. The sounds were slow and deliberate, as if someone were trying to get around without being noticed. A chill ran down his spine. The sense of panic that was never too far away in his daily life quickly rose to the surface. *Not tonight,* he whispered under his breath. *Please—no threats tonight.*

Louis leaned against the wall near the door and listened as the footsteps entered the secretary's office next door. His heart pounded fiercely in his chest, and his breathing became rapid. He couldn't take it anymore. He couldn't stand there and be a target. He'd have to confront her.

Gathering up his courage, Louis stealthily entered the dark hallway. He moved slowly, with his back against the wall. The office was only a few feet away. The door was opened a crack, and a faint light was shining out into the hallway. Louis edged his way to the office, then waited outside the door.

He listened. It was silent, except for the sound of his own breathing. Louis held his breath, trying to quiet the sound, but it only made him gasp for air. The sound seemed so loud to him that he was sure his breaths were echoing down the long, dark hallway. It would be so easy for her to find him.

You have to go inside, he told himself, despite being frozen with fear. *On the count of three, you will go inside the office and face her once and for all.* Beads of sweat trickled down his forehead. He felt like a child who had just woken up from a terrible nightmare. *One . . . two . . . three.* In complete terror, he pushed open the door and jumped into the room.

No one was there. Everything in the secretary's office was in its place, except for the small desk lamp that someone had left on. Louis reached out, steadying himself against a row of faculty mailboxes, and tried to catch his breath. He was relieved but angry at the same time. He despised living in constant fear. And it was all her fault. She had made him that way.

It was then that Louis noticed the letter in his mailbox. He'd checked his box just before Stark left, and it had been empty. But now there was a small white envelope waiting to be opened, ready to expose the threats. He wasn't crazy after all. She *had* been there.

Louis's hands shook as he broke the envelope seal. *Why are you doing this to me?* he thought as he tore into it nervously. He unfolded the letter and realized instantly that it wasn't her handwriting. It was Jessica's.

He read the letter. Jessica was writing to apologize for what had happened at the beach. He was touched by the emotion in her note. His fingers traced the letters of her signature. Louis felt the muscles in his body suddenly relax, but his heart was heavy. It would be wrong to let her get mixed up in his crazy life. He had no other choice. Staying away from Jessica was going to be the hardest thing he ever had to do.

Chapter Fifteen

"Professor Stark? This is Winston Egbert. I'm sorry to be bothering you at home—" Winston stopped short. He suddenly had the sinking feeling that he'd just made the biggest mistake of his college career.

"What is it, Winston?" the professor asked sternly.

Winston took a deep breath. *It's too late now; just go ahead and ask him.* "As you know, sir, I've been making a real effort to turn in my work on time. Now that I've proved how hard I'm willing to work, I was hoping you'd consider giving me some extra help for the exam."

"I have been pleased with your effort, Mr. Egbert, although I'm wondering if maybe it came along too late in the semester," the professor said.

Winston's palms started to sweat. He could feel Stark's disapproving glare through the telephone.

"Please, sir, you said that if I turned in my work, you'd help me."

"I believe what I said was that it was useless for me to take the time to show you things you should have picked up by doing the homework," he answered pointedly.

Winston's insides felt like they were collapsing. Obviously Professor Stark had already made up his mind, and it would take nothing short of a monsoon to change it.

"Furthermore, I'm afraid your approach to learning is backwards, Mr. Egbert," the professor continued. "You seem to do only what is necessary to get by until the next exam. Once the exam is over, you let things slide until the next time around. Instead your goal should be to *learn,* which means a constant commitment to your work. I know you think it takes up too much time, but ironically, your way actually takes up more."

Calling him at home was definitely a bad idea, Winston decided. Stark must have known how awkward Winston was feeling, and he was probably enjoying every painful minute of it.

"I understand exactly what you're talking about, sir, and I promise to study that way for the next exam. But that isn't going to help me for this one. My parents are going to kill me if I get a bad grade on this test. You're the only one who can help me."

Professor Stark chuckled. "I had a feeling there must be a greater force motivating you. Still, I have to admire your persistence," he said, sounding almost friendly for once. "To reward you for your tenacity, I'm going to grant you your wish. I will write up a short list of topics you should concentrate on for the exam."

Winston's heart leapt for joy. "Thank you so much, sir," he gushed.

"I won't be in my office Monday because I will be in faculty meetings for most of the day. But Professor Miles should be there to let you in. I'll leave a copy of the study guide on my desk."

"I really appreciate this, sir. You don't know how much this is going to help," Winston said.

"You're welcome, Mr. Egbert," Stark answered coolly. "But keep in mind that this is only a study guide. The rest has to come from you."

"Don't worry," Winston said, smiling to himself. "It will."

Elizabeth turned down the brightly lit hallway of Todd's dorm building and couldn't believe what she saw. Todd was slumped against the door of his room, his eyes glassy. There was blood on his face and hands, and his dark suit was covered with mud. Elizabeth ran to help him.

"Todd, are you all right?" Elizabeth shouted. She put her arm around him to help him stand up.

"Yeah . . ." he said groggily. His eyes rolled to the back of his head and then started to close. Elizabeth was afraid he'd slip out of consciousness. She opened the door and eased him into his room.

"What happened?" Elizabeth asked as she sat him down. She grabbed a towel and gently wiped the blood off his face.

Todd's breathing was labored. "Two guys jumped me," he said weakly. Elizabeth touched his nose, and Todd winced.

"It's not broken, is it?" she asked worriedly.

Todd closed his eyes. "I don't think so." He took off his necktie and looked down at the mud that covered his arms and legs. "They ruined my suit."

"Don't worry about the suit. We'll have it cleaned." Elizabeth opened his mini-refrigerator and took out some ice. She worked quickly, wrapping the handful of ice in a towel. She handed it to him. "Do you know who did this to you?" Elizabeth asked as she reached for the phone.

Todd pressed the cold pack against his cheek. "They were dressed in black. I couldn't see a thing."

Elizabeth dialed a number and put the receiver to her ear. "I'm calling Mr. Santos to cancel the appointment. I hope we can reschedule soon."

"Not too soon," Todd said. "Wait a few weeks so my bruises can heal."

Elizabeth let the phone ring several times, but there was no answer.

"I can't believe this," she said, slamming down the phone. She gave him a clean towel for his nose. The bleeding was slowing down. "Is there any chance that the people who did this don't want you back on the team?"

"It has nothing to do with that, Liz," Todd said slowly as he cleaned the mud from his wounds. "It has to do with the investigation."

Elizabeth's jaw fell. *What?*

"They said we'd better drop the investigation or else. Apparently we're close to the truth and someone doesn't like it," Todd said. He tilted back his head to stop his nose from bleeding. "Maybe Tom is right—we *don't* know what we're doing. Let's call him and ask his advice."

"No—absolutely not!" Elizabeth said stubbornly. "I want to do this without his help."

"Liz, now is not the time to prove a point. It's getting dangerous."

Elizabeth didn't answer. *Who could be doing this? Who would go to such extremes to keep us from discovering the truth?* Obviously it was someone who was deeply involved in the scandal. And judging from the severe beating they gave Todd, they had an awful lot to lose.

Elizabeth looked at Todd guiltily. She'd had no idea that asking him for help would get him into so much trouble. "I'm calling Gin-Yung," she said, picking up the phone again. "You need her."

"Don't," Todd said quickly. "I don't want her to know about it."

"But she's going to see the bruises—"

"I don't want her involved. If she knows anything, she might end up getting hurt," he said thickly. "Maybe we should *all* stay out of it, for that matter."

207

Elizabeth gingerly placed the receiver back in its cradle. "Look, Todd, I can completely understand if you want to back out of this. But I'm not dropping it. I'm not going to let those bullies get away with beating you and whatever else they're trying to cover up."

Todd put down the ice pack. "Don't get any crazy ideas in your head, Liz. It's over. You don't have to prove anything to anyone," he said earnestly. "Sometimes you need to know when to throw in the towel."

Never, Elizabeth thought as she forcefully brushed the dirt off the sleeves of his suit.

"The essays were good for the most part, but next time try to be a little more creative." Louis walked up and down the center aisle of the classroom as he handed back the papers. "Don't rush through the assignment just to get it done—put your heart into it."

Jessica shifted in her seat. Her heartbeat raced as she waited for her grade. *Did he get my note?* She studied his face, trying to find something in his expression, some clue to tip her off. He continued to circle the room in his usual professional manner, passing out papers and giving comments to the students. It felt like an eternity. One more minute and Jessica thought she was going to burst.

Louis turned and walked down the aisle with the last essay in his hand. Jessica nervously looked down, scribbling meaningless words in her notebook. She saw the toes of his brown leather shoes stop directly in front of her desk.

"Nice work, Jessica," he said, dropping the paper on her desktop. Jessica looked up and smiled faintly. His eyes were glowing.

Jessica waited for him to leave before looking at her essay. Each page was covered with comments in red ink. She impatiently scanned the notes, then turned to the back page. He gave her an A-. Below the grade was a note: *See me after class.*

Jessica's heart soared. He liked her work and thought she had done a good job. And now he wanted to speak with her. *This is a good sign,* Jessica thought confidently. Writing the note was a good idea after all. He must have forgiven her. She watched the hands of the clock move slowly around the dial. There was only half an hour left in class, but to Jessica it felt like forever.

At the end of the lecture Jessica bolted to the front of the room. Louis was already surrounded by students who were bombarding him with questions about the essays. Even though they were swarming around him, Louis noticed Jessica. He motioned for her to come to the other side of the desk. Jessica stood beside him.

"Just a minute," he said to the students, who were all talking at once. He turned and smiled at Jessica. "Here are the keys to my office," he said, handing them to her. "I'll be there in a few minutes."

Jessica clasped the keys tightly in her hand and floated out of the room.

Elizabeth ate a forkful of salad and went over the list of evidence. The cafeteria was crowded and more noisy than usual, but she hardly noticed. She was too absorbed in her investigation. There was so much left to do—so much that she still didn't understand. And now that Todd was no longer helping, it was going to get a lot harder.

"Do you mind if I sit with you?"

Elizabeth looked up to see Gin-Yung standing next to her. "Please do," she said with a smile. Elizabeth cleared a space for her.

"I thought I'd never find a place to sit," Gin-Yung said gratefully. "But this worked out well. I was kind of hoping we could have a talk."

Elizabeth closed her notebook. Judging from the serious look on Gin-Yung's face, Elizabeth had a pretty good idea what she wanted to talk about. "Did you see Todd?" she asked.

"Finally, this morning," Gin-Yung answered. Her face looked tired. "Todd loves crullers, so I brought him some to celebrate the meeting with Mr. Santos. But when I got there, he only opened the door a crack. He wouldn't let me inside."

Elizabeth speared another forkful of salad. She had been afraid this would happen. How long did Todd think he could hide the truth from his girlfriend?

"After a while, I finally talked him into letting me inside," Gin-Yung continued. "I saw the bruises. He said he never went to the meeting with Mr. Santos. Then he told me some wild story about getting hit in the face with a basketball—but that's not what really happened, is it?"

What should I do? Elizabeth wondered. Todd *did* ask her not to tell Gin-Yung because he wanted to protect her. Even though Elizabeth disagreed with it, that was still his decision. While she never intended to approach Gin-Yung, Elizabeth hadn't counted on the fact that Gin-Yung might come looking for her. Did that mean she had to lie for Todd? "I'm not sure. . . ." she answered vaguely.

Gin-Yung rested her elbows on the edge of the table. "Please, Elizabeth. I know something is going on. And you two have spent so much time together—you must know something," she pleaded. "Todd's shutting me out completely. He won't tell me the truth. He's acting like I can't handle it."

Elizabeth knew how she felt. Tom had been treating her the exact same way. Elizabeth looked into Gin-Yung's dark eyes and decided that it was time she knew the truth.

Gin-Yung listened to the whole story, from beginning to end, without blinking an eye. "I can't believe he kept this from me," she said ironically. "Especially since sports is my specialty."

Elizabeth nodded apologetically. "I'm sorry I didn't come to you sooner," she said.

"It's all right—I forgive you," Gin-Yung answered with slight smile. "But I hate being left in the dark."

211

Elizabeth threw down her napkin and pushed her tray to the side. "So now that you've heard the facts, what do you think about the case?"

Gin-Yung removed the lid from her container of strawberry yogurt. "Actually, I've seen this kind of thing before. Something like this happened in my high school."

Elizabeth leaned forward anxiously. "What is it?" she asked.

Gin-Yung looked around stealthily, then leaned toward Elizabeth. "Point shaving," she whispered. "I'd bet ten to one that two and a half million didn't come from alumni. It came from some sort of gambling ring."

Elizabeth sat back in her chair, letting the information sink in. "Are you telling me that someone is paying SVU players to control the point spread?"

Gin-Yung nodded. "Exactly. What happens is, a gambler bets huge sums of money that a team will win by a certain margin, then he pays the top players on the team to guarantee the outcome. That way, the gambler's bet always come in. It's as simple as that."

Elizabeth's head was reeling. "What do you know about Daryl Cartright?" she asked.

Gin-Yung ate a spoonful of yogurt. "I remember doing a write-up on him in the paper. He was a freshman point guard with the highest assist-to-turnover ratio anyone had ever seen. He also had a knack for three pointers."

"So why did they get rid of him?" Elizabeth asked.

Gin-Yung shrugged. "His performance fell. But it was kind of fishy. At the start of the season, his foul shots were around 90 percent. By the fourth game, he was down to 40 percent. Short of an injury, a major change like that is pretty suspicious."

Gin-Yung had read Elizabeth's mind. The pieces were starting to fall into place. This scandal was going to be even bigger than they'd originally thought. It was going to be the story of her career.

Elizabeth was seized by a new sense of determination. If only she could break it before Tom came back. He'd never doubt her abilities again.

Chapter Sixteen

Winston knocked on the door several times, but there was no answer. He tried to turn the knob, but the door was locked. Stark had said Professor Miles would be around to let him into the office, but he wasn't there. Winston hoped he'd show up soon—he needed that study guide as fast as he could get his hands on it.

Winston sat heavily on the bench outside the office. No one was around, not even a janitor with a master key. *Just one more day and this will all be over.* Winston sighed. His eyes burned from studying, and his head was filled to capacity with theories and formulas. Everything he needed to know for the exam was sloshing around in his brain like a thick, murky stew. Winston seriously doubted his mind would be clear enough to answer the questions on the test.

The study guide was his last chance. All he'd

have to do was spend the rest of the time cramming for the topics on the guide, and he'd ignore everything else. Then, in less than twenty-four hours, he'd take the exam and be finished with this.

A tired smile crossed Winston's face at the thought of seeing Denise again. Maybe she'd even be waiting for him outside the auditorium after the test and they could go to lunch. It had been so long since they'd spent any time together, he almost forgot what it was like to be with her. She was probably already getting used to not having him around. He hoped her feelings for him hadn't changed.

Winston's thoughts were interrupted by the sight of Jessica Wakefield as she turned the corner and stood in front of the office door. There was a strange, contented look on her face.

"The door's locked," Winston said.

Jessica smiled brightly. "I know." She fished a key out of her pocket and unlocked the door.

Winston jumped to his feet. "Where did you get that? You're a lifesaver."

Jessica opened the door to the office and switched on the overhead lights. She took a seat in the chair next to Professor Miles's desk.

Winston followed awkwardly behind. "Professor Stark is supposed to leave me a study guide . . ." he said, pointing to the desk. He ambled over to it and discreetly looked at the papers sitting on the desktop.

Jessica seemed too busy to care. She was holding a small mirror compact and was combing her fingers through her blond hair. Winston started looking through the papers with more confidence. Finally he spotted the study guide in the upper corner of the desk.

It was a single sheet of paper. At the top were the words THIS IS WHAT YOU NEED TO STUDY written in bold black letters. Below were the words *Everything from page 1 to page 175.*

"This must be some kind of a joke," Winston said out loud. He flipped over the sheet of paper. On the back was written, *Mr. Egbert—Hope you're more prepared for the next exam.*

Winston angrily crumpled the paper into a ball and hurled it into the wastebasket. Professor Stark had tricked him. He knew Winston would rely on the study guide to pass his exam, and he had punished him for it.

Winston's chest heaved as he tried to breathe. Now he would definitely fail, his parents would find out, he'd have to go to another school, and he'd never see Denise again. He was wrong to think it would all be over after the exam tomorrow. It was just the beginning of a long and miserable life.

Jessica opened the office window, and a gust of cool air filled the room. It was raining outside. Winston was trudging hopelessly on his way out of the office when a piece of paper blew off Stark's desk and onto Winston's foot. He picked it up with agitation. Suddenly he realized he was holding a copy of tomorrow's test.

Winston froze. His first thought was to look away. *Just take a peek,* a little voice whispered in his ear. Temptation overcame him, and his eyes scanned the test. He read and reread the questions over again, but they made very little sense to him. There was no way he'd be able to memorize it.

Unless, of course, he took a copy with him.

Put it down and walk away, Winston told himself sternly. He put the paper back, but he couldn't get his feet to move. They were planted firmly in place.

Pick it up, the voice whispered. Winston ran his fingers over the paper. It was so easy. All he had to do was take it with him, and no one would ever know.

You can't do that, Winston told himself. He pulled his hand away. It was cheating. It was wrong.

All your problems will be solved. Winston thought about how hard he'd been working, and how little of it was actually sinking in. Studying had become a game—it had less to do with him caring about grades, and more with him needing to be with Denise. Winston touched the corner of the paper.

It's cheating.

No one will ever know.

Winston looked around, then tucked the copy of the test into his shirt pocket.

Jessica loved the smell of rain. Especially a cool spring shower mixing with the green scent of the freshly cut lawn out on the quad. It was incredibly romantic. Jessica leaned slightly out the window, imagining she was on an iron balcony and that the walkway below was a busy Paris street.

A drop of rainwater fell on her nose, and Jessica moved back inside and closed the window. She brushed the dampness from her face. As she turned around, she expected to see Winston Egbert, but instead she saw the amused face of Louis.

"It was a bit warm in here . . ." Jessica said, blushing.

"You can leave it open if you want to," Louis said gently. "I love rain too."

Jessica opened the window again. She smoothed the wrinkles in her black rayon mini-dress and took a seat, gracefully crossing her legs.

Louis looked at her for a long moment, his hands dangling easily off the edge of the armrests. "You've done marvelous work in this class, Jessica. I'm really proud of you."

"Thanks." Jessica looked down humbly. She could feel his eyes on her, like that day at the water fountain. *He's going to kiss me,* she thought ecstatically. She could see it in his eyes.

His forehead creased, as if he were suddenly lost in thought. "But there is something we need to talk about, and it doesn't have anything to do with your work."

Jessica nodded. She felt a tingle in her stomach, then it spread throughout the rest of her. She was suddenly very glad she had written the note. She couldn't tear her eyes away from his mouth. The thought of Louis finally kissing her made her lips tremble.

"I got your letter," Louis started slowly. The corners of his mouth drooped a bit, and his brow was furrowed. Jessica sensed that he was probably nervous too. "I'm sorry I was abrupt with you at the beach. I didn't mean to hurt your feelings."

"It's all right. I understand," Jessica said, her voice swelling with emotion. This was it. This was the moment she had been longing for.

"But there's much more to it than that. As I read your note, I suddenly realized something." Louis's tone became flat. "It seems that a boundary has been crossed, and I want to make sure it doesn't happen again."

Jessica wanted to reach for him, but she held back. "That's why I wrote the letter—I know I never should've asked such personal questions. It'll never happen again, I promise."

Louis looked directly at her. His eyes were clouded, like the Pacific before a storm. "Jessica, I don't think you follow what I'm saying. I'm your teacher, not your friend. If I ever gave you the wrong impression, I'm terribly sorry."

Jessica's throat tightened, and she struggled for air. She looked away. The sight of his beautiful lips blinded her, as if she were looking into the sun. "But you're . . ." Her voice faltered. *You're wrong!*

219

Louis shook his head. "I should have seen this coming long ago."

Liar. Her entire body burned with the fire of humiliation. Tears sprang to her eyes. *You're wrong. You're a liar.* She wanted to kick and scream, to make him feel the same pain she was feeling right now.

"I'm always here if you need help with your work, but I'm afraid—"

Before she could hear another word, Jessica ran out of the office.

"The moving brigade has arrived!" Magda shouted as she walked through the door of Lila's room. Several Thetas followed in tow, carrying empty cardboard boxes and paper bags.

Lila laughed. "I thought you guys would never show up. Did you honestly expect me to do this all by myself?"

Isabella opened a small cardboard box filled with tea cakes. "We had to stop for some refreshment," she said, opening a quart bottle of iced tea. "Thetas can't get any work done unless they have some sort of gastronomic motivation."

Lila looked around at what was once her dorm room. Clothes were piled high, like colorful haystacks, all over the floor. Cosmetic cases, shoe boxes, art books were all scattered about. Her vanity case and matching bureau were tucked away safely in the corner.

Thetas had gathered around the box of tea

cakes, chatting about the latest gossip. Lila stood on her bed and clapped to get everyone's attention.

"Okay, everyone, listen up." She waited until all eyes were on her before she continued. "Everything needs to be put away carefully in boxes. The clothes on the left side of the room are washable, the right side are dry clean only. Please don't mix the two." Lila pointed to the respective piles. "The furniture is off limits. And by the way, everything in that box near the windowsill is up for grabs."

No sooner were the words spoken than suddenly there was a mad rush to the other side of the room. A few Thetas fell in the scramble, landing on soft piles of dry-clean-only fabrics.

Alison was the first one there. "I got a bottle of French perfume!" she shouted excitedly.

Kimberly snagged a tube of lipstick and some mascara. "Thanks, Lila," she said.

Lila plopped down in a chair. "Anything for my sorority sisters," she said grandly. Lila leaned back her head and looked up at the ceiling. "Did anyone bring a ladder?"

"I did," Denise said. She stepped out into the hallway and came back with a wooden stepladder. "What do you want me to do?"

Lila pointed to the ceiling. "I need you to take down those glow-in-the-dark stars." She had bought the stars right after she and Bruce had been rescued from their terrible ordeal in the Sierra Nevada. That was when they'd started to fall in love. Every night, when they were trying to stay warm in the wilderness, Lila would look up at the stars in the sky. When she got home, Lila made Jessica put them up on the ceiling, exactly as she had remembered seeing them in the mountains. Ever since Lila went to bed under the glow of the stars, with the memory of Bruce's strong arms around her.

Denise climbed the stepladder and reached for one of the stars.

"Wait a minute!" Lila shouted, lunging for her.

Denise nearly fell off the ladder. "What is it?" she asked.

Lila tore through the piles of clothes on the floor, mixing dry clean with regular laundry. Finally she came across her camera case.

Everyone stopped and looked up. "These must be the famous wilderness stars I've heard so much about," Isabella said with a laugh.

Lila snapped a picture. "You can laugh all you want, but it's important that I know exactly where to put the stars in our new place."

Isabella started to fold a stack of blouses. "Lila, your ceiling is so high, you won't be able to see them from the bed."

"I'll put them under my canopy, then," Lila said resolutely. She gave Denise a nod. "You can continue. Put them in an envelope, and *be careful*."

Magda tried on a pair of earrings that were in the giveaway box. "I heard your new place is totally spectacular. When are we going to see it?"

"As soon as we're moved in and the interior decorators fix it up a bit," Lila said, her eyes flashing with excitement. "Then I thought maybe we'd invite you all over for a dinner party."

"That sounds fun," Alison said, spritzing herself with perfume.

Isabella sat down in a chair next to Lila, holding a flat cardboard box in her lap. "We're really going to miss having you around, Li." She reached over and gave her a hug.

Lila's eyes were moist. "I'm going to miss you guys too."

"We all got together to give you a little moving-off-campus present." Isabella handed her the box.

Lila looked up at everyone and smiled. She lifted the lid and carefully pushed back the tissue paper. Inside was a small quilt, made of different-colored *T*'s that had been sewn together. Each *T* was signed by a different Theta sister and had a personal message.

Lila started to cry. Thetas swarmed around her, giving her a group hug. "This is so sweet. Thank you all." Lila looked at the names on the quilt. In the center of it was a blue-green *T* signed by Jessica. It said, *I wish both of you much love and happiness. And I expect full hot-tub privileges. Love, Jess.*

Lila looked around. "Is Jess coming?"

No one seemed to know. Isabella shrugged. "I haven't seen her all day."

Chapter Seventeen

"Jessica, wait!" Louis called as he watched her storm out of the office. He sank back into his chair, covering his face with his hands. The rain poured steadily outside, and in the distance there was the low rumbling of thunder.

Louis shivered. He didn't believe a word he had said to her. The whole time, all he could think about was taking her into his arms. He wasn't trying to be mean; he was only trying to save her from heartbreak. But that was exactly what he had given her. He wished he had never spoken to her that night in the bookstore. They could have avoided all this. Jessica deserved so much better.

Louis walked over to the window. He opened it as high as it would go and stuck his head outside. Wet, heavy drops landed on his hair and trickled down his shirt collar. He saw Jessica leave the building, her head bent low and her books clutched to her chest.

"Jessica!" he shouted at the top of his lungs. People were looking up from the walkway below. Rain pelted him like daggers. "Jessica!"

She didn't stop, and she didn't turn around. She only kept running. Jessica was running away from him, running out of his life forever. And there was nothing he could do to stop her.

"This is it," Elizabeth said as she steered the Jeep down Maplewood Lane. The rain was coming down in sheets now, and the puffy gray clouds had turned an ominous blue-black.

Elizabeth turned her windshield wipers on as fast as they would go. Luckily the address wasn't too far from campus. Regardless, it would have taken a hurricane to keep her from making the trip. There was simply too much at stake.

Elizabeth felt the flutter of nervousness in her stomach. Thanks to Gin-Yung's job at the campus newspaper, she had managed to locate Daryl Cartright's current address. If he cooperated with her, she could be well on her way to breaking open the scandal. Elizabeth glanced down at the directions in her hand. According to Gin-Yung, Daryl lived in the fourth house on the left.

It took Elizabeth only a moment to know that Gin-Yung was right. There was a basketball hoop bolted to the side of the one-car garage, and a yellow foul line was painted on the driveway. The house was a modest, one-story ranch, with white siding and green-painted shutters. It was simple, nothing out of the ordinary. It didn't look like the house of someone who was involved in a heavy-duty gambling ring.

Elizabeth parked across the street and stayed inside her Jeep while the rain poured down outside. It didn't look like anyone was home. She suddenly wished she had called first, at least to tell him she was coming. But Tom had taught her never to do that. His golden rule for investigative reporting was never to give your interviewees a chance to prepare their answers. It was better to take them by surprise.

A tall young man with red hair came out the side door of the house. Elizabeth recognized him instantly. Daryl was wearing shorts and an SVU tank top, and he dribbled a basketball. He seemed completely unfazed by the rain. Elizabeth watched as he tossed the ball effortlessly into the basket from the foul line. She was amazed at how easily he moved for someone with such height. He had grace, speed, and complete control of the ball. Daryl took several steps back and shot again and again, the ball sinking into the net without touching the rim every single time. No matter what the athletics department said, Daryl Cartright was far from mediocre.

Elizabeth stepped out of the Jeep and walked toward the driveway, holding an umbrella over her head. She hoped he'd be willing to talk to her. He was her only hope.

"Daryl Cartright?" Elizabeth asked. She stepped aside as he ran past.

Daryl dunked the ball into the basket. He wiped his hands on his wet jersey. "Yes?" he said, out of breath.

She looked up and extended her hand. "My name is—"

"Elizabeth?"

Elizabeth turned toward the side door of the house, where the voice was coming from. Standing there, dressed in sweats, was Todd.

"What are *you* doing here?" Todd asked in surprise.

Elizabeth looked at Daryl, then back at Todd. "I was just about to ask you the exact same thing."

Jessica heard thunder in the distance. Her face was soaked, but she couldn't tell if it was from the rain or from her tears. The cold raindrops poured down, making the gauzy material of her dress cling to her body. Her hair fell in wet, twisted ropes.

Her only instinct was to keep walking. She moved like a robot, one foot in front of the other, not knowing where to go. Moving was the only thing that could numb the pain. She wanted to continue on forever, without stopping, until she was as far away from Louis as possible.

Jessica felt a small tremor deep inside her. It was icy cold, moving, gaining momentum. It was the lie that Louis had told her. He'd said he had no feelings for her, that it had all been a misunderstanding. For a moment, Jessica almost believed him. She swallowed the words whole, letting them move around inside her as if they were the truth. It shook her, with a chill that penetrated her bones.

Jessica hugged herself as her body began to shake uncontrollably. *How could I let this happen?* Tears streaked her face like a frozen river. Jessica wanted the chill to reach her heart so that she would never allow herself to love again.

A flash of lightning burst overhead, and a crack of thunder split the atmosphere. Jessica trudged along slowly, the cushions of her sandals completely saturated with rainwater. A silver Toyota drove past her, spraying mud onto her legs as it passed. Jessica didn't stop.

The Toyota stopped several feet in front of her, then started to back up. It inched closer and closer to her, and Jessica continued to move forward. It seemed as though nothing and everything was happening at once.

When she was near the car, the driver rolled down the window. "I've been looking all over for you," he said. "Let me give you a ride back to campus."

Jessica lifted her wet head and looked inside. It was Louis. She didn't answer. Her teeth started to chatter. She moved away from the car and continued walking on.

Louis drove alongside her. "You must be freezing. Let me bring you back to your dorm," he said in a gentle voice.

Lightning flashed. "No!" she shouted. "Go away!"

"Please, Jessica . . ." he said, his voice breaking. "Don't be mad at me. I wasn't trying to hurt you."

A chill ran through her. Jessica looked away.

"Please forgive me," he said softly.

The warm tone of his voice turned her head. Louis's eyes were liquid. They held all the pain that she felt inside.

"Let me give you a ride back," he said.

He opened the door for her, and Jessica stood there for a moment, looking at it. She got into the car.

A wave of warmth hit her. Jessica couldn't stop the flood of tears. It was as if all the ice that had moved inside her were suddenly beginning to melt. She looked down at the dashboard, trying to control her sobs.

Louis brushed the tangled wet hair from her face. "I'm so sorry," he whispered.

Jessica stared into his eyes. They were glistening with tears. He took her into his warm embrace, and Jessica cried. The coldness, the lies all drained out of her. In their place she was filled with the sweetness of his smell, the heat rising up from him, the gentle way his fingers caressed her cheek.

Louis slowly lifted her chin with his fingertips.

Jessica responded instantly to his touch. She tilted back her head and parted her lips slightly. Then the passionate fire of his kiss came down upon her.

Ecstasy. Pure and total ecstasy.

Will Jessica and Professor Miles become an item? Find out if Louis will risk his career for love in Sweet Valley University #16, **DEADLY ATTRACTION.**

SIGN UP FOR THE SWEET VALLEY HIGH® FAN CLUB!

Hey, girls! Get all the gossip on Sweet Valley High's® most popular teenagers when you join our fantastic Fan Club! As a member, you'll get all of this really cool stuff:

- Membership Card with your own personal Fan Club ID number
- A Sweet Valley High® Secret Treasure Box
- Sweet Valley High® Stationery
- Official Fan Club Pencil (for secret note writing!)
- Three Bookmarks
- A "Members Only" Door Hanger
- Two Skeins of J. & P. Coats® Embroidery Floss with flower barrette instruction leaflet
- Two editions of *The Oracle* newsletter
- Plus exclusive Sweet Valley High® product offers, special savings, contests, and much more!

Songs from
the Hit TV Series

Featuring:

*"Rose Colored
Glasses"*

"Lotion"

*"Sweet Valley High
Theme"*

*Available on CD and Cassette
Wherever Music is Sold.*

Life after high school gets even *Sweeter!*

Francine Pascal's
SWEET VALLEY
SVU
UNIVERSITY
Life after high school gets even sweeter.

Jessica and Elizabeth are now freshmen at Sweet Valley University, where the motto is: Welcome to college — welcome to freedom!

Don't miss any of the books in this fabulous new series.

♥ College Girls #1	0-553-56308-4	$3.50/$4.50 Can.
♥ Love, Lies and Jessica Wakefield #2	0-553-56306-8	$3.50/$4.50 Can.
♥ What Your Parents Don't Know #3	0-553-56307-6	$3.50/$4.50 Can.
♥ Anything for Love #4	0-553-56311-4	$3.50/$4.50 Can.
♥ A Married Woman #5	0-553-56309-2	$3.50/$4.50 Can.
♥ The Love of Her Life #6	0-553-56310-6	$3.50/$4.50 Can.
